W9-DCV-518

"Go adead. Search me," Ava challenged Carson.

Anticipation flared in Carson's eyes. A slow, devil-may-care smile spread on his lips. Warmth heated Ava's cheeks, and suddenly she doubted directly challenging a man like Carson Nash was the best approach. A man who operated in the black and the gray, outside the law.

Carson raised her chin with his fingers, his touch less than forceful, but more than casual. He brushed his lips against hers, sending a torrent of heat through her body. Ava sucked in a breath attempting to cool the fire in her veins, but it wouldn't be doused. She gazed up at him, caught in the moment and lost in a hazy memory of the two of them that she couldn't quite grasp. Placing a hand on her stomach, feeling for movement from their unborn child, drew her to him in a way that seemed familiar.

His assault on her emotions continued. In one urgent move he pulled her into his lap and kissed her again. Leaning back, she turned her head toward Carson's ear. "Stop this now."

"Oh, but I can't. Not until I find what I'm after."

JAN HAMBRIGHT

AROUND-THE-CLOCK PROTECTOR

HARLEQUIN®

TORONTO • NEW YORK • LONDON
AMSTERDAM • PARIS • SYDNEY • HAMBURG
STOCKHOLM • ATHENS • TOKYO • MILAN • MADRID
PRAGUE • WARSAW • BUDAPEST • AUCKLAND

If you purchased this book without a cover you should be aware that this book is stolen property. It was reported as "unsold and destroyed" to the publisher, and neither the author nor the publisher has received any payment for this "stripped book."

ISBN-13: 978-0-373-88814-6
ISBN-10: 0-373-88814-7

AROUND-THE-CLOCK PROTECTOR

Copyright © 2008 by M. Jan Hambright

All rights reserved. Except for use in any review, the reproduction or utilization of this work in whole or in part in any form by any electronic, mechanical or other means, now known or hereafter invented, including xerography, photocopying and recording, or in any information storage or retrieval system, is forbidden without the written permission of the publisher, Harlequin Enterprises Limited, 225 Duncan Mill Road, Don Mills, Ontario, Canada M3B 3K9.

This is a work of fiction. Names, characters, places and incidents are either the product of the author's imagination or are used fictitiously, and any resemblance to actual persons, living or dead, business establishments, events or locales is entirely coincidental.

This edition published by arrangement with Harlequin Books S.A.

® and TM are trademarks of the publisher. Trademarks indicated with ® are registered in the United States Patent and Trademark Office, the Canadian Trade Marks Office and in other countries.

www.eHarlequin.com

Printed in U.S.A.

ABOUT THE AUTHOR

Jan Hambright penned her first novel at seventeen but claims it was pure rubbish. However, it did open the door on her love for storytelling. Born in Idaho, she resides there with her husband, three of their five children, a three-legged watchdog and a spoiled horse named Texas, who always has time to listen to her next story idea while they gallop along.

A self-described adrenaline junkie, Jan spent ten years as a volunteer EMT in rural Idaho, and she jumped out of an airplane at ten thousand feet attached to a man with a parachute just to celebrate turning forty. Now she hopes to make your adrenaline level rise along with that of her danger-seeking characters. She would like to hear from her readers and hopes you enjoy the story world she has created for you. Jan can be reached at P.O. Box 2537, McCall, Idaho 83638.

Books by Jan Hambright

HARLEQUIN INTRIGUE
865—RELENTLESS
943—ON FIRE
997—SHOWDOWN WITH THE SHERIFF
1040—AROUND-THE-CLOCK PROTECTOR

Don't miss any of our special offers. Write to us at the following address for information on our newest releases.

Harlequin Reader Service
U.S.: 3010 Walden Ave., P.O. Box 1325, Buffalo, NY 14269
Canadian: P.O. Box 609, Fort Erie, Ont. L2A 5X3

CAST OF CHARACTERS

Carson Nash, a.k.a. Marathon—Leader of IAops, a secret team of CIA agents. He's in charge of a hostage rescue mission, but when he discovers the hostage is a CIA attaché he had a relationship with, can he protect her and overcome his past in order to have her in his future?

Ava Ross—She's supposed to be dead after the plane she was on crashed. Although she's resurfaced, she has no memory of Carson Nash, the man who claims to be the father of her unborn child.

CIA director Glendow—He's Ava's boss, but where do his loyalties truly lie?

Jerome Hinshaw—A brilliant MIT student who has vanished. Are his research and the microchip he produced key to the IAops mission?

Doctor Gary Resnick—A man Carson trusts. He's ex-CIA with a closet full of mind experiments. Did he use one of them on Ava?

Mark Jarrett, a.k.a. Nitro—He's the team sniper and the go-to guy for anything that explodes.

Cyrus Hunt, a.k.a. Joker—He might be the team's comic relief, but you'd definitely want him on your side in a crisis.

Nick Shelby, a.k.a. Domino—A former master of disguise, he's good at his job, but there are things in his past he'd rather forget.

Eli Carico, a.k.a. Tux—This diplomatic affairs expert looks good all dressed up and under fire.

Luke Haden, a.k.a. Doc—Suffering from a guilt trip after a mission gone wrong, he's sitting this one out on Maui.

Chapter One

Agent Carson Nash raised his night-vision scope and stared through the lens into the darkness.

Near the front entrance of the rustic log cabin, nestled in a grove of white pine, he picked up movement.

He dialed in the targets—two armed guards, shooting the breeze instead of paying attention.

Changing his focus, he scanned the side of the cabin, his gaze settling on a window void of curtains.

Light shone from inside the room.

He zeroed in on a single individual.

"Bingo," he whispered into his headset mic. Their objective was still alive. He'd been tied to a chair. A black hood pulled over his head made him unidentifiable.

"All units. The package is being held in the northwest corner bedroom. There are two, I repeat, two armed bogeys at the front entrance."

"Copy that, Marathon. We'll set up for extraction."

The hostage turned his head in response to something outside Carson's view.

A man clad in a suit entered the room, smoking a cigarette.

Adrenaline pulsed in Carson's veins.

He swung the scope back toward the front of the cabin, getting a new fix on the guards.

This mission seemed too easy. The directorate had given IAops the logistical coordinates, including a dead-on estimate of the number of bogeys they'd encounter. The only thing he didn't know was the agent's name.

Caution raked his nerves. It was a simple hostage rescue, something he and his team had done dozens of times. They'd secure the agent, transport him back into the fold, where the CIA could deal one-on-one with the possible security breach.

"Marathon, we're in position."

"Copy that, Domino. Stand by."

Carson panned back to the bedroom window.

The man in the suit was still in the room. Still circling the agent, his jaw flapping rapidly as he spoke.

The captive shook his head in response to his captor's words.

The man stopped and raised his hand, but stopped short of striking the hostage.

Anger hissed in Carson's veins. As much as he wanted to rain retribution down right now, he was powerless to stop the abuse. They had to wait until the agent was alone, or risk a human shield situation. Something he wouldn't do.

"Hold up, Domino. The sight picture isn't clear."

Seconds stretched into minutes. Tension knotted the muscles between his shoulder blades while he watched and waited for the bogey to leave the room.

The man pulled something from his jacket pocket.

Carson trained his focus on the activity,

watching him raise a clear vial and shove a hypodermic needle into it, drawing the plunger down.

The man removed the needle and grasped the agent's arm. The agent flinched, and his head drooped forward.

Whatever he'd been given had put him out in seconds.

The bogey pocketed the paraphernalia and left the room, closing the door behind him.

"Domino. You're clear to go."

"Copy that, Marathon."

Carson listened for the sounds of his men's swift annihilation of the enemy.

He had to smile when Nitro's voice came over his earpiece. "The fun and games are over."

"Copy. I'm on the move. Nitro, we'll take the front. Domino, Tux, you've got the rear. Joker, hostage protection."

"Roger that," said Agent Cyrus Hunt, also known as Joker.

Carson eased out from behind the prickly tree and moved into position, pausing next to the front door.

Nitro, aka Agent Mark Jarrett, stepped out of the darkness and took up a ready position on the opposite side of the entry, a flash-bang grenade in his fist and a grin on his face.

"It's a go," Carson whispered into his mouthpiece.

In one fluid motion he raised his leg and jammed his boot into the front door.

It burst open.

Nitro tossed the device into the house.

They took cover beside the doorway.

The percussion grenade exploded.

Smoke belched from the doorway.

Glass shattered at the side of the house, signaling that Joker had entered the room where the agent was being held.

"Go-go-go!" Lunging forward, they rushed into the cabin, using the commotion as cover.

Resistance came in the form of the man Carson had seen administer a shot of something to the agent.

In one swift move Carson side-kicked the man in the solar plexus.

He flew backward into a chair, his eyes wide with surprise.

"Stay put," Carson commanded, backed

up by Mark Jarrett, who trained his 9 mm on the bogey.

"All clear," Agent Eli Carico said as he stepped through the haze, followed by Agent Nick Shelby.

"Round everyone up," Carson ordered. "See who they work for."

Eli Carico grinned. "My pleasure."

He didn't doubt it. Eli could make a tight-lipped thug spout like a shaken can of soda.

"Don't have too much fun. There has to be enough left to put detain in detainee."

"You got it." Eli and Mark escorted the man outside, where he'd join his fellow bogeys for a round of questioning.

The smoke from the flash-bang grenade cleared as Carson entered the room where Agent Cyrus Hunt stood next to the uncon-scious hostage.

"I saved the unveiling for you. This here is a real surprise package."

"The guy in the suit Mark and Eli escorted outside shot him up with something just before we hit. He has a syringe in his jacket pocket and the bottle the drug came out of. See what it is."

"Copy that, but this hostage isn't a he." Cyrus left the room, a grimace on his face.

Carson studied the restrained agent dressed in black from head to toe, his gaze eventually settling on narrow feminine ankles just above female-issue service flats.

"Damn." He felt sick as he untied the cord that held the black sack over her head.

He loathed anyone who would brutalize a woman, and he had the scars to prove just how deep his conviction ran.

Carson pulled the hood off, releasing a mound of hair the color of burnt mahogany.

Disbelief pounded inside his brain.

He went to his knees in front of her, sliding his hand under her chin, he raised her head. Need, instant and uncontrollable, jolted his body.

Staring into her face, he mentally traced the line of her jaw, allowing his gaze to settle on her mouth. He remembered the taste of her lips on his.

He lowered her chin to her chest and released her, caught off guard by the heat that crept up his arm and fanned out through his body.

He knew her, but in the rift between reality and fantasy, he struggled to bridge the chasm with the facts he'd been given months ago.

Carson stood up, every muscle in his body cranked tight.

Agent Ava Ross was legally, physically and categorically dead. She'd died four months ago in a plane crash. He'd read the damn dossier himself, but he'd just made a positive ID, right down to the tiny mole on her right cheekbone.

She was still alive, flesh and bone, and a hell of a long way from Annandale, Virginia, the last place he'd seen her before her overseas assignment.

"Joker, do you copy? What was in the hypo?" he said into his open headset mic, wishing to hell his chief medical expert, Luke Haden, was in the forty-eight, instead of nursing a guilt trip on Maui with a bottle of Jack Daniel's.

"Copy, Marathon. The vial contains lorazepam."

Relief coursed through him. Lorazepam was a mild sedative. She'd come out of it soon, depending on the dosage.

"Copy that. Come back and sit with Agent Ross."

"I'll be right there," Cyrus said into his mouthpiece. A moment later he appeared in the doorway of the bedroom and stepped inside. He covered his mouthpiece. "Did you say Ross, as in Ava Ross? You worked diplomatic detail with her in D.C. for a couple of weeks right after our mission in the Middle East."

"Yeah. She was serving as an attaché to Borisov."

"She's supposed to be dead."

"That's what I thought." Carson watched curiosity slide across the face of his number two man.

"We need to get her out of here. I don't like the feel of this operation. What's the word on the bogeys?"

"Russian."

He glanced down at Ava. What did the Russians want from her? The fact that they were holding her as a hostage proved they knew she hadn't been aboard the downed aircraft along with their ambassador.

He would make it his mission to find out

why. He only hoped he could live with the answers when he discovered them—and he would, all physical attraction to her aside.

"Let's get her back to the warehouse. She's got no apparent injuries, but she needs a head-to-toe assessment. We'll take it from there."

Carson untied the ropes binding her body to the chair.

She fell forward into his arms.

He scooped her up. The physical contact drove hot shards into him, superheating the blood in his veins as he carried her out into the living room. He was conscious of another time when he'd done the same, only her bedroom had been his target destination, and the contact skin on skin.

With the military precision of a drill sergeant, he hammered his thoughts into line and positioned Ava on the sofa.

"We'll take the bogeys back to the warehouse. You can work your magic on them there." He glanced up at Agent Eli Carico.

"I'll get the van." He pulled open the front door, looked side to side and vanished into the night.

Agent Nick Shelby sauntered out of another bedroom with a laptop computer in his hands. "They've been talking to someone. I'll take this apart at the Lazy-B lab, see what I can find." He put the laptop down on the dining-room table next to a window and opened the computer. "How's your Russian, Hunt?"

"Better than yours, Romeo," Cyrus said, a broad grin on his face. "Tatiana helped me brush up."

"I'll bet she did." Agent Shelby gave him a smirk. "Was that before or after you gave her a submarine lesson?"

"Knock it off. Let's clear the scene, package the targets for transport and get the hell out of here," Carson ordered, unsure why his men's banter had set his nerves on edge. Normally it had the opposite affect.

"I'm on it." Cyrus sobered and left the cabin, closing the front door behind him.

The air inside the small room sagged with tension.

Carson tried to shake it off, but couldn't. Something wasn't right—he could feel it in his gut.

Glancing out a side window, he caught a glimpse of movement in the trees at the edge of the perimeter lined with pine and buck brush.

His agents doing their jobs—nothing scary about that, unless you were the target.

Caution worked through him as he trained his stare on Ava. She appeared peaceful in her drug-induced slumber. What had she gotten herself into?—or out of?—he wondered.

She'd been one of the top attachés to Russian ambassador Yuri Borisov, who'd died in the plane crash four months ago along with his entire entourage.

A plane she was supposed to be on.

But here she was, a hostage in a small cabin high in the Cascade Mountains of Washington State. It was a hell of a long way from the wreckage, tanked at the bottom of the Bering Strait, three thousand miles away.

The first sniper bullet came through the window next to Agent Shelby and blew apart the laptop computer on the table next to him.

The second round bored into the wall on the opposite side of the room.

Carson lunged for the light switch next to the front door. The cabin went black.

A barrage of gunfire echoed through the trees.

"Nick! You okay?"

"Yeah. Where the hell'd that come from?"

Carson belly-crawled to the sofa and pulled Ava down onto the floor next to him. "East side of the cabin."

Yanking his 9 mm out of its ankle holster, he jacked a bullet into the chamber and came to his knees.

"All units, do you copy? We're under fire." Tension coiled his muscles into knots as he waited for a response, wishing he'd gone with his gut and ordered his team out sooner.

"Copy, Marathon." Agent Mark Jarrett's reply hissed into his earpiece. "We're pinned down seventy-five feet from the cabin. We can't get a fix on the sniper."

"Copy, Nitro. Where are the bogeys?"

The pause was deafening.

Carson's gut fisted.

"They've been hit."

Carson pulled in a breath. "Condition?"

"Code black."

Dead.

Anger rattled him. There'd be no hard and fast answers tonight. "Copy that, Nitro."

Another burst of gunfire split the darkness. Several rounds thudded into the cabin's thick log walls and shattered the remaining windows, sending a spray of glass into the room.

Carson dropped onto Ava, covering her body with his own. "Tux. What's your location?"

Eli Carico's voice came over his earpiece. "I'm in the van, headed your way."

"Copy. Hold up. Joker, Nitro, make your way down to the road and rendezvous with Tux. Nitro, I need some fireworks at ten-second intervals."

"Copy that. The fourth of July's coming early."

Carson braced for the show. Agent Mark Jarrett was never one to spare the bang.

"Did you copy, Domino?" Carson asked.

"Loud and clear," Agent Shelby whispered into his mic from near the table where he'd taken cover.

The minutes passed, marked by short bursts of gunfire outside in the woods.

"Marathon, fire in the hole. I'll wait for your go."

"Copy." Carson felt Ava move under him. He rolled off her and came to his knees. "Rendezvous at Tux's location. Let me know when you get there."

"Copy that."

The gunfire intensified, assuring Carson his men were on the move. So far he'd counted seven different rounds of weapons fire. They were outmanned and outgunned. If they didn't vacate the site—and soon—they'd be overrun.

"Marathon, we're on top of the vehicle. Orders?"

Carson scooped Ava into his arms and crawled on his knees to the back door.

"Roll up to the rear door on the third blast. We'll make a break for the van."

"Copy that."

Agent Shelby joined him at the back door, the remains of the laptop under his arm.

"It's a—" Carson said into his mic, but

the explosion came before he could give the full order.

The cabin rattled.

"Sorry, Marathon. My finger got happy."

"Beats the hell out of a dud." Carson pulled Ava closer, mentally preparing for their escape as he counted off ten seconds.

Blast number two was close. Its percussion shook the tiny log structure like a 6.0 quake.

Six…five…four…three…two…one.

Explosion number three ignited. The ground shuddered, rattling the dishes in the cupboards.

"Go-go-go!" Carson yelled.

Nick Shelby threw open the rear door, his pistol raised.

The van ground to a halt, raising a cloud of dust.

The side door slid open.

Carson made a lunge for the opening.

A bullet zinged past, just missing his head.

Their escape had been spotted. He only hoped the opposition didn't have reinforcements waiting down the road.

They made it to the vehicle just as all hell broke loose with detonation number four.

"Hang on," Eli shouted from the driver's seat.

"I'm hit!" Nick yelled as Mark and Cyrus pulled him into the van and shut the door.

"Location?" Carson asked, cradling Ava against him.

"My leg."

"Cyrus, check for bleeding."

"Can do."

Carson tried to relax as Eli spun the van around and peeled out of the driveway.

"Any sign of backup for these thugs?"

"Negative. I didn't see anyone along the road."

He felt a breath of foreboding as the van sped down the narrow dirt road leading to the main highway and escape.

"Did you get anything from the bogeys before lights-out?"

"Yeah. The man in the suit was a doctor," Cyrus said from the rear seat. "I didn't get a chance to check the other two's credentials before the sniper took them out."

Concern laced through him. Why would

there be a Russian doctor on scene, unless he'd been there to make Ava talk? He knew some Russian agents used psychological alteration and warfare. Had she become a victim of their cruel methods? And what possible information could she have that would be of any value to them? She was an attaché. Top secret wasn't in her job description.

Carson gritted his teeth as the van lurched hard to the right, almost knocking him over.

"Take it easy, Eli. We're in the home stretch."

"Have a look out the rear window."

In the distance and closing fast, a pair of headlights on high beam bored into the back of the van.

Could this mission go any more wrong? Carson wondered as he settled Ava on the floor next to him and drew his pistol.

"Give this crate all you've got."

"Can do." Eli accelerated.

"Have you got more poppers, Nitro?"

"Are you kidding? I buy them by the truckload."

"Let's give our pals a display they won't forget."

"Coming right up." Mark unzipped his pack and dug in.

"How's Nick?" Carson asked.

"He'll live," Cyrus said. "A bullet grazed his calf. I can clean it up at the warehouse."

"No offense, but I'm going to the hospital," Nick said, his voice strained from the pain. "Dr. Heidi Fields is on call tonight. I checked. One look at her and a man's pain moves to another location on his body. I might get lucky tonight."

"A guy like you can hope." Cyrus chuckled, a broad smile on his face, shadowed in the headlights of the car behind them.

"It's ready. What do you say we turn this babe loose?" Mark crawled to the rear of the van, put his hand on the door handle and popped the latch.

He pushed it open a crack and dropped the explosive out. "Three…two…one."

The C4 exploded as the car drove over it.

A fireball lit up the night sky.

The driver swerved, lost control and slammed into a tree.

Eli hit the brakes.

The van slid to a stop.

Carson stared out the rear window at the smoldering car. "Back it up. Let's ID these guys."

Eli put the van in Reverse and backed toward the accident, stopping twenty feet shy of the car.

"Keep your eyes open and your weapons handy," he ordered.

Like the expertly trained assault team they were, they dispersed as they left the van, taking up their positions in precision as they approached the disabled vehicle.

"Clear," Carson said into his mouthpiece as he stood next to the driver's window staring at the two unconscious men inside the black sedan.

He pushed the driver back from the air bag and steering wheel. Reaching inside the man's lapel pocket, Carson pulled out his ID and flipped it open, turning it toward the red glow coming from the van's taillights.

A picture of the driver stared up at him from an NSA security badge.

"What the hell…they're NSA."

Carson stared back up the road leading to the cabin, his body tense.

"Search the car for weapons. Let's see if they were doing the shooting tonight."

A warning pounded in his brain.

What were a couple of National Security Agency spooks doing in the middle of a CIA hostage rescue operation?

Chapter Two

Carson reran the mission in his head on the ride back to the warehouse in Issaquah.

The team had done everything right, but having Ava passed out in the seat next to him added to the grind of uncertainty wearing down his clarity.

He was a CIA man. No questions, no regrets, but he couldn't deny the fact that they'd been sent on the mission minus the players list.

Until he knew exactly what they were dealing with, he planned to take countermeasures.

"I'm ordering the team dark for twenty-four hours," he said as the van slowed and the gate to the warehouse swept open. Once he returned Ava to McLean, they'd rendezvous back at the Lazy-B in Idaho.

"Use it for some personal downtime."

"Reason?" Cyrus asked from the rear of the van.

"Call it overreaction, call it gut garble, but until we know what those two NSA spooks were doing in our wagon train, we're better off scattered. We'll hitch the team back up after I deliver the package and debrief."

"You won't get an argument from me," Cyrus said. "Something's going on. We'll probably be the last to know."

"Maybe." Wariness pinched the muscles between his shoulder blades as Eli stopped the van in front of the warehouse's overhead door and pressed the opener.

"Watch your backs," he said, staring into the warehouse, which was illuminated by the van's headlights.

One by one the team pulled and readied their weapons. If the hostage rescue had been compromised, there was always a chance the warehouse was no longer secure.

"Nitro, Joker, Domino, take the flanks.

Tux and I will take it straight up the middle in the van. Copy?"

"Loud and clear," Agent Hunt said.

Mark, Nick and Cyrus exited the vehicle through the side door and slipped inside the open door, disappearing into the shadows outside the headlight beams.

Carson's heart rate picked up as he waited, prepared to take on whatever might come at them from out of the darkness.

"All clear, Marathon," Agent Hunt said.

"Copy that, Joker."

Eli pulled through the door just as the overhead lights came on. He stopped the vehicle and killed the engine. "Need help getting her into the office?"

"I've got it. Thanks." Carson lifted Ava and climbed out the side door. He stared down at her in the harsh glare of the fluorescent lights overhead.

Her color had returned, but still he was worried. An overdose of any sedative could be fatal, and they had no way of knowing how much had been administered.

He headed for the secure room at the back

of the building. One by one his men filtered in from their search-and-secure mission.

Once inside the enclosed office, he strode into the back room they used as sleeping quarters, hit the light switch with his elbow and laid her down on his bunk.

He straightened and looked at her. A wave of longing rose inside him. What had happened between them months ago had been spontaneous, but that indiscretion had the potential to cause them both a lot of grief.

The agency frowned on personal relationships between operatives, and physical contact of a sexual nature was strictly off-limits. The temptation could end one's career. Still, that threat hadn't been enough to cool their desire or keep them from jumping into the fire with both feet.

Heat burned through him, warming his blood again. He gritted his teeth and left the room, closing the door behind him.

His men were busy stuffing gear into their packs.

"How is she?" Cyrus asked, looking up from his task.

"Still out, but her color's returned and her breathing is steady."

"Want us to hang around?"

"Negative. She's not a threat. I'll deliver her and make contact in twenty-four hours. Make sure you and the team recover whatever you can get from the laptop."

"Okay." Nick picked up his pack and slung it over his shoulder. Giving the rest of the team a nod, he left the office.

One after the other, his men walked out of the room and then the warehouse, disappearing like ghosts at dawn. Each with his own silent agenda, a protocol trained into them. A protocol that could someday save their lives.

Carson hung his head as the warehouse lights went out, leaving the cavernous building hollow and silent.

He closed the door to the office and punched the lock-down code into the keypad.

In a matter of seconds steel shutters slid down over the windows, encasing the room in a layer of protection. He didn't know exactly who the enemy was, but they hadn't found a single rifle in the NSA agent's car. Whoever had done the shooting at the cabin and taken out their bogeys was still out there, and if they were lucky enough to pinpoint the warehouse, they'd play hell trying to get inside.

Carson hesitated at the door to the sleeping quarters. He needed to do a head-to-toe medical assessment on Ava, but the thought of touching her again spilled fire into his veins.

She was a hostage. A hostage he'd been directed to rescue and return to the fold. His mission was almost complete. He'd have her back at CIA headquarters in twelve hours.

Reaching out, he turned the knob and pushed the door open.

Carson stopped in his tracks.

Something was wrong.

He'd left the light on in the room and now it was dark. He glanced at the bed where he'd put her down.

It was empty.

"Ava? It's Carson Nash. I'm coming in so you can tell me what happened to you, and where you've been for the last four months."

Silence greeted his words and hung in the air. Caution worked through him.

Listening, he tried to pinpoint her location in the small room. There was a hidden escape hatch, but the code was locked in his head. Still, there were plenty of places to hide.

"Come on. We haven't got much time." He stepped forward, determined to locate her. Determined to get answers.

"Ava?"

The force of the metal door caught him full in the face, sending him backward.

He managed to stay on his feet, and recovered his balance in an instant.

Lunging forward, he rammed the door with his shoulder before she could get it closed.

She shrieked.

The note of fear in her cry sliced into his mind, taming the primal, all-or-nothing response he'd been conditioned to unleash on his opponent.

"I'm coming in!" He pushed against the door, feeling her resistance wane.

The door swung open.

He stomped into the room, anger evident in his steps.

Turning to the left, he spotted her pressed into the corner, but it was the small .32-caliber handgun she pointed at him that made him pause. She'd found his hideaway pistol, tucked into the box springs of his bed.

Staring at her, he tried to name the emotion in her moss-green eyes, but couldn't. What the hell had happened to her?

"Put the gun down."

He took a step toward her. Her eyes widened in panic.

Compassion filled him. "You're safe here. We're in a secure location. I just want to talk to you before I take you back to McLean."

The panic in her eyes turned to terror. She took two steps back. "I won't go! Who are you?"

Surprise rattled him. He stared into her face, intent on discovering the Ava Ross he knew existed somewhere inside the haggard and frightened woman who pointed a lethal weapon at his chest.

"Agent Carson Nash. CIA. IAops. We met

in D.C. four months ago. I've been directed to rescue you and return you to the fold."

"I know you?" The raspy question sent a charge of concern through him. He stepped closer.

"We worked a diplomatic detail together." If the information registered at all, it didn't show. Instead, confusion glistened in her eyes.

She'd been altered—he was sure of it. Concern jolted him into action. "Come on, Ava. Give me the gun. I need to make sure you're okay."

"Don't come any closer. I know how to use this."

He didn't doubt it for a minute. She'd been able to keep up with him at the firing range, nailing him shot for shot.

"The Russians holding you drugged you. Do you know what they gave you?"

"Drugged?" She shook her head in denial. "Bastards!"

With each passing second she became more agitated. He had to get the gun before she tapped him. Maybe he could talk her down with facts.

"My team and I rescued you from a cabin in the Cascade Mountains. We brought you here, but there were snipers on scene. If you don't put the gun down and let me help you, we might have to deal with them again."

He watched her soften, but not melt.

"I want to leave. I want out of here." She glanced around, sidestepping out of the corner. "You're going to take me home. Do you understand?"

"And where is home?" Carson studied her, watching her struggle for an answer.

"I…" A single tear squeezed from her eye and streaked down her cheek.

Sympathy looped around his nerves. Ava Ross had been compromised. With drugs, hypnosis, he wasn't sure, but he had to get her to a doc.

"Outside D.C. You have a nice place in Annandale with a great patio. We barbecued steaks. Don't you remember?"

She stared at him, her beautiful eyes becoming hollow and lifeless. "I don't believe you. You want to hurt me and my—"

"You're wrong." Carson stepped toward her, determined to end the situation. He wore body armor under his shirt. He could survive a gunshot if he took it straight on. It was a risk he'd have to take.

"No closer! Do you hear me—don't come any closer. I'll shoot, I swear to God I will."

Carson braced for live fire and charged her, catching her around the waist.

The gun went off.

A bullet sang past his ear and pinged into the ceiling, but he held on to her, pushing her back with his momentum until they collided with the wall.

She grunted, the impact driving the air out of her lungs.

He grabbed her right wrist, pulled her arm up over her head and pinned her with his body.

The contact seared him. "Look at me, Ava," he demanded, intent on searching out a glimmer of recognition in her hollow stare. But her gaze was blank, her thoughts unreadable.

With his right hand he took the pistol away from her and let her go, taking a step back.

"I don't want to hurt you, but it's obvious you've been altered."

She turned and stumbled to one of the beds, where she sat down. "Do you have credentials?"

Carson snagged his agency ID from the desk next to the bed and flipped it open.

She stared at it for a moment before gazing up at him to confirm that the picture and the man were one and the same.

She swallowed. "You called me Ava. What's my last name?"

"Ross. Agent Ava Ross." A knot coiled in his gut. "We worked together in D.C., but that's not important right now. I need to know what happened to you. You were supposed to have died four months ago aboard a Russia-bound aircraft, along with Ambassador Yuri Borisov. I read the dossier."

Ava rocked forward, putting her head in her hands. "I wish I could help you, Agent Nash, but the last thing I remember is getting in a limo for the ride to the airport on March first at eight in the morning. Nothing days before, and sketchy details after."

"Were you in the car alone?" Carson tensed. From her bedroom window he'd watched her get into the limo that morning after a night of mind-bending sex.

"There was someone else in the car, but I can't remember who it was. I've tried."

"So the last four months of your life are missing?"

"More or less." She looked up at him, her eyes brimming with tears.

Carson popped the clip out of the gun and put it on the desk. "I know someone in Seattle who might be able to help you recover your memory before I transport you to McLean."

She stood up, her body stiff with tension.

"What is it? What's wrong?" In four steps he was next to her.

"I can't go there. I don't know why, but I can't go there. Please." She stared at him. Her face contorted into a grimace, her eyes pleading.

"The directive has come down. I'm bound to honor it."

Reaching out, she locked her hand on his forearm. "You don't understand. I can't go there. They'll hurt me. They'll hurt—"

"Shh." Carson stared up at the signal light in the corner of the room. It flashed in rapid succession, warning him trouble was on the way.

"Someone's trying to penetrate the outer security curtain. We don't have much time." He grabbed the gun from the desk and reinserted the clip.

Taking her hand, he led her into the outer room, where he grabbed his pack, shoved the gun inside and killed the lights.

"There's an escape hatch."

She followed him back into the sleeping quarters.

Carson paused in front of the closet and pulled open the door. Reaching around the jamb, he found the control panel and turned the release, disguised as a coat hook.

Ava jumped as the rear of the closet slid open, revealing a steep stairwell.

"We've got ten seconds." He pulled her into the closet, closed the door and stepped through the opening, taking her with him.

Pausing on the landing, he turned and pressed the control panel. The portal closed, and the emergency lighting system came on overhead.

"I don't know how they found this place,

but there's a chance they know about this escape hatch."

"Who are they?" Ava asked as they made their way down the narrow stairs and into a long hallway.

"I'm not sure. Could be Russian, could be NSA. This whole damn mission is stacked up like rush-hour traffic on the pike."

He picked up the pace, breaking into a jog, still holding Ava's hand. "They could be waiting at the other end of the corridor."

Ava's heart rate skyrocketed as Carson rushed her along the escape route. Her breath came in deep gasps that seared her lungs and made her feel light-headed.

"Stop…please, I can't…" Her legs refused to move. Only the force of Carson pulling her along kept her forward momentum going, until her knees buckled and she hit the floor in a rush of black.

"Ava! Ava!"

The feel of his hand against her cheek snapped her back into the light. She stared up at him, feeling a brief moment of familiarity circulate through her mind.

"I can't run anymore."

"Then I'll carry you."

Ava closed her eyes, letting the darkness cover her anxiety. She had to tell him.

Opening her eyes, she looked up into his chiseled face. It was a handsome face, the face of a warrior. She could see it in the hard set of his jaw, in the intensity of his stare, in the deep scar above his left eyebrow.

Something in the feel of his rough worn hand against her cheek spoke of intimacy, of a crack in the rock-hard fortress training had built around him.

But could she trust him? Did she have a choice?

"I've got a problem," she whispered.

A look of concern flashed across his face, breaking the mask of determination he wore.

"I should have done a medical assessment. Are you hit?"

"I know exactly what's wrong with me, and a physical assessment won't make any difference. The outcome will be the same."

He stared at her, confusion in the narrow squint of his vivid blue eyes.

"It's nothing five months won't cure."

Men, she thought as she gazed up at Agent Carson Nash. So necessary, but clueless at times. "I'm pregnant, Agent. At least, that's the diagnosis they gave me at the free clinic. Four months along."

Carson felt his last gulp of air lodge in his lungs. He didn't have to do the math to realize the impact of what she'd said.

He swallowed, trying to keep his head in the game. Could the child be his? The night they'd spent together four months ago flashed by in his mind and he knew the answer.

"We have to keep moving. I'll carry you." Carson pulled Ava to her feet, steadying her against him.

"I can walk."

He put his arm around her waist and moved forward, spotting the end of the escape route. The exit door was still three hundred feet away and to the right, where it opened at the surface in an abandoned junkyard.

Worry bit into him. There was a vehicle at the other end, gassed and ready to go. He had to be prepared for the possibility of an onslaught from the enemy, and the chance that the rig had been compromised.

They hit the end of the corridor and took a hard right.

Carson stared at the exit. Protecting Ava and her baby had become paramount the instant she'd told him she was pregnant. The fact that the child could be his made it that much more critical.

He pulled up short next to the door and released her. "Once we get out, there's a blue pickup a hundred feet straight ahead of the exit. The key is under the driver's seat. The front gate will open automatically when you fire the engine. I want you to get out of here and take I-90 into Seattle. Get on the 5 South to Tacoma."

Carson pulled a pen and paper out of his pack. "When you get there go to this address. I have a buddy, a doctor who can help you recover your memory."

"What about you?" She stared at him.

Carson gritted his teeth. "Look. If we walk into a firefight and I don't make it out, I want you to go. Do you understand?" He pressed the name and address into her palm.

"Ava! Promise me you'll go. You have a child to think about."

Unshed tears brimmed in her eyes. "I promise."

"Good, now put this on." He pulled off his shirt, exposing the bulletproof vest he wore underneath.

"I can't take it. You need it. You're breaking protocol."

"To hell with protocol! Listen to me. You can't move as fast as I can. I'll keep them busy. Get to the truck and head for the front gate. Don't stop until you clear it. I'll be there."

Ava shook her head. "What if I pass out again?"

Carson put the vest over her head and fastened the buckles, pulling them tight. "You're a good agent, Ross. You're not going to pass out. You're going to get the damn truck and we're going to get the hell out of here. Do you understand?"

She stared up at him. Fear and uncertainty glimmered in her eyes.

"Do it for your child." An odd sense of desperation spread over him as he focused on her face. Short of wrapping himself around her, he was dependent on her own grit, her own need to protect her baby and herself.

She squared her shoulders and shoved the paper into her pants pocket. "You'll tell me more about our meeting when this is over?"

"Yeah." Carson's muscles cranked tight as he stared at the woman he was duty bound to protect.

The woman carrying his child.

Chapter Three

"Use this if you have to." Carson pulled the pistol out of his pack and handed it to her, fighting a degree of hesitation. He'd just turned over the same gun she'd trained on him moments ago, but he wouldn't leave her defenseless to save his own skin.

She took it from him. "I'm ready."

Drawing his 9 mm from its ankle holster, he pressed the exit code into the keypad.

The locking mechanism disengaged and the heavy metal door gaped open an inch.

He stared through the crack, watching for movement among the abandoned vehicles in the junkyard beyond the safety of the escape tunnel.

"Looks clear."

Ava listened to Carson explain how they

were going to get to the pickup. Somewhere in her mind she knew what he was saying even though the words and tactics were foreign to her. Her instincts and muscle-imprinted training had surfaced more than once tonight. She just prayed it would all come out if she needed it again.

"Where's the truck?"

Carson pointed out a Ford pickup parked between a Chevy Suburban and a large box truck with U-Haul painted above the cab.

"Indirect route?"

"Yeah," Carson said.

She glanced at him, catching a twinkle of admiration in his blue eyes. A shiver of familiarity rippled through her. Frustrated, she shuffled the fragmented memories in her head, hoping she could draw the one that included him, but it was as elusive as a Las Vegas card trick.

"Take the left side. If we draw fire it'll be from the gate entrance."

Her nerves bunched. "Let's go."

"Nice and slow." Carson eased the door open and took her hand. Together they stepped outside into the darkness.

The only light in the junkyard rained down from a mercury vapor lamp next to the front gate.

Carson pushed the door shut, cutting off their retreat. There was only one way out now.

"Stay behind the line of cars next to the fence. It's your best cover if they start shooting."

She nodded, dropped down into a crouching position and moved away from him.

Carson watched her disappear into the shadows. He broke right, working his way to the string of cars closest to the gate. The spooks on their trail seemed to have inside information.

If they knew about the warehouse there was a chance they knew about the escape hatch. They'd probably penetrated the security curtain by now and were scouring the office.

He paused next to a rusted-out truck, searching for signs of movement among the junk cars next to the fence.

His eyes locked on Ava and he followed her progression toward the pickup. She was a smart woman. Stealthy and capable.

A brief instant of admiration zipped through him, but it was short-lived, killed off by the sound of the exit-door lock mechanism.

He turned toward the sound, his pulse thumping in his ears.

The door eased open, revealing five men dressed in black. One by one they scattered like spiders and blended with the surrounding darkness.

The hair at his nape bristled. He tried to pinpoint their individual locations, getting a fix on four of them, but number five had moved out of his field of vision.

Foreboding hammered his nerves. Refocusing, he searched for Ava in the darkness.

She had a head start and the brains to keep it.

Staying low, he moved forward, working his way closer to the front gate.

In the distance the distinctive creak of a vehicle door in need of oil put hope in his gut.

The seconds ticked by as he waited for the sound of the truck engine. Without it, the front gate wasn't going to budge.

To his left, the murmur of voices set his nerves on edge. He listened intently. English. No accent. They had to be CIA or NSA.

Moving cautiously, he edged closer to the voices, trying to make out what they were saying, but the night went still as he peered out from behind a wreck.

Ping! A bullet ground into the car a fraction of an inch above his head.

Carson dropped back and scrambled to the rear of the vehicle for cover.

He'd been spotted. They were minutes away from an all-out assault.

Rising a fraction, he pulled the trigger, raining a hail of bullets in the direction the shot had come from.

The thugs returned fire, giving up their locations.

In his peripheral vision on the left he saw movement.

Turning, he pumped two rounds into one of the thugs and watched him drop.

Lunging forward, he hit the ground and rolled several times, coming to his knees at the rear of two cars.

A streak of black charged forward between the vehicles.

Carson double tapped him, and pulled forward to a position twenty-five feet closer to the pickup.

Where the hell was Ava? She'd had plenty of time to fire up the rig.

Worried, he tried to spot her location, but the lighting was blocked by the box truck.

Was she okay? Had man number five gotten through his defenses somehow?

Concern turned to determination as he crept closer. Staring into the darkness, he saw her head bob up from below the pickup's dashboard.

One of the thugs had managed to work his way around the nose of the U-Haul.

Dammit. Carson laid down a blaze of gunfire and charged forward, zigzagging back and forth, bent on reaching the pickup before the spook did.

But he was too late.

Ava's muffled screams ground over his nerves as he rushed the last fifteen feet, oblivious to the gunfire coming in from behind.

Bolting to the passenger side of the pickup, he reached inside and grabbed the man.

Carson yanked hard, pulling the attacker into his arms. Fueled by instinct and training, he locked his head in a death grip and snapped his neck.

Ava's blood turned cold in her veins. She stared at Carson, afraid to breathe. He'd just killed a man without a moment's hesitation.

She felt a slice of fear as he shoved the man aside and jumped into the pickup.

"Get out of here! There are two more where he came from."

"I can't find the key!" Panic consumed her.

"Try the visor!" he shouted.

An onslaught of bullets pinged into the pickup.

Carson hung out the side window and returned fire.

Ava's hand shook as she pulled the visor down.

The key ring fell into her lap like a gift from heaven.

She felt for the ignition. Finding the keyhole, she shoved the key in and turned it over.

The starter ground.

Backing off the key, she turned it again, pumping the gas pedal in a frantic effort to get the pickup to start.

"Take it easy—you'll flood it."

She gritted her teeth and turned it again.

The engine roared to life.

"Go-go-go!" Carson ordered.

Ava popped the truck into gear and stomped on the gas pedal.

The pickup shot out of the parking spot spewing dirt and gravel into the air.

Cranking the wheel hard to the left, she aimed for the gate, now only a quarter of the way open.

"Don't stop! Ram it!" Carson shouted from the seat next to her as a bullet entered the cab and exited the driver's window in front of her face.

Shooting for the narrow opening, she pushed the pedal to the floor.

The sickening grind of metal on metal penetrated her hyped-up senses as they squeezed through the opening in a shower of sparks.

Slamming on the brake, she turned the steering wheel hard to the right, skidded out onto the highway and floored it.

She reached down and pulled on the headlights less than a quarter of a mile from the junkyard.

"Where to?" she asked, backing off the accelerator and bringing the truck speed down to 75 mph.

"We're five miles from the freeway on-ramp. Pull over when you see the first I-90 sign. I'll take the wheel."

"Okay." She glanced over at Carson as they passed under a streetlight.

Her heart froze in her chest.

"You've been hit!"

"It's a scratch. I'll live."

Panic made her nerves feel perforated as she gauged the amount of blood soaking the right side of his shirt. "You need an E.R."

"It's a flesh wound. I'll patch it up. It's more important we stay ahead of the spooks who just tried to kill us."

Her nerves calmed a bit, but blood was

bad, spooks or no spooks. She'd met the macho, ain't-nothing-but-a-scratch type before…hadn't she?

Glancing into the rearview mirror, she searched the highway behind them for headlights.

It was clear. They weren't being followed, so far anyway.

She let out the breath she'd been holding and tried to relax.

The miles ticked by and before she knew it she spotted the I-90 sign Carson had said would be there. "This is it," he said.

Slowing, she pulled the truck off into a turnout next to the highway and stopped.

Carson climbed out the passenger side and came around the front of the pickup, pausing next to the driver's door. Pain sizzled along his rib cage, stinging like an SOB.

It was a flesh wound, but the bullet had probably bruised his ribs. Gritting his teeth, he pulled open the door as Ava slid across the bench seat onto the passenger side.

He climbed in and put the truck in gear, pulling back out onto the highway. "Nice piece of driving."

"Thanks. At least I remember how to drive." The hopeless note in her voice sliced through the barriers he'd erected to survive. He'd felt hopelessness in his life, and it wasn't a good vibe.

"The doctor in Tacoma can help. He's the best."

"Who are you…really?"

Carson glanced at her in the back glare of the headlights. There was no disguise for the leery gleam of mistrust in her eyes.

"IAops. I'm supposed to bring you into the fold in one piece."

For a brief second her features softened. "You did give me your vest. It was a stupid move. It would have saved you from that bullet."

The air between them felt charged as he focused on the road ahead and the freeway entrance sign.

"Why did you give me your vest? You broke protocol."

"I like to bring my packages in alive." The answer was honest. As honest as he could afford to be with her.

"Is that what I am? Your package? How

do I know you're not taking me in for more of the same thing I've just survived?"

"You don't." Carson stared straight ahead, feeling a torrent of tension move in waves around them, sucking the conversation into deeper water.

If she became uncooperative he'd have his hands full. Moving a combative individual cross-country would make his job more complicated. Then there was the baby inside her. His baby, most likely.

Carson swallowed, determined to take control of the situation before it turned ugly.

He needed her cooperation. Needed to know what had happened to her and where she'd been for the past four months. He needed to know what she knew about the child she was carrying.

"Your baby. Who's the father?" He gave her a sideways glance.

Her profile was unreadable as she stared straight ahead. "I don't know. I've tried to remember who was in my life at that time, but I can't." The desperation in her voice tugged on his moral code, leaving him torn.

Was it possible the information could

bring to light her memory of the night they'd spent together before her disappearance? Maybe that one detail would spark more memories. Memories of where she'd been, who'd taken her and why.

He worked the scenario over in his head, dancing around the one revelation that could strengthen or weaken his position with her.

"I gave you my vest to protect you…and your child."

"To protect your mission, you mean? God forbid you don't complete your mission. I've heard about you Black Ops types. Admit it, Agent Nash, you don't care about the collateral damage."

He felt guilty. It was true. The mission took priority. Without its completion, he'd failed, mentally…physically.

"I want out," she said.

Carson glanced sideways, catching a glint of light on the barrel of the stainless steel .32 he'd given her in the junkyard.

His nerves stretched tight as he fought the instantaneous violent response that had been trained into him.

"I want you to drop me at the police

station when we get to Seattle." Her voice
wavered, belying the certainty in her
request.

Carson let up on the gas pedal. The
pickup slowed.

"What are you doing? Don't stop. I'll
shoot you."

"You'll have to, because I'm not going to
take you to the cops. You belong at
McLean."

"I can't go there!"

He pulled the truck onto the shoulder,
stopped and turned toward her.

"You have to trust me, Ava."

Tears welled in her eyes and glistened in
the glare of the dash lights. He watched a
myriad of emotions flow across her face,
but she didn't lower the gun.

He couldn't risk hurting her—he'd have
to talk her down.

"You were with someone the night before
you got on that plane."

She stared at him, a muddled look of disbelief and relief on her tear-streaked face.

"You were with me. There was no one
else in your bed. You told me yourself."

"I don't believe you!"

"I've got proof." Slowly he reached toward his pants pocket.

"Stop! Don't try anything."

"Relax." He dug in to his pocket, keeping his eyes on her. Finding the crumpled business card he'd almost thrown out a hundred times, he pulled it out and opened it.

"We spent the night together. You gave this to me the morning after we—"

"Are you saying…"

"The child you're carrying is mine."

Chapter Four

"You're lying!" Ava tightened her grip on the pistol, the only thing holding Agent Nash at bay. Doubt raked her thoughts, turning them like fall leaves.

She stared at the business card in his fingers, fighting to grasp even a wisp of a memory, but she kept coming back to the same conclusion.

He was an agent, intent on bringing her in. He'd say and do anything to accomplish his mission.

Her moment of hesitation evaporated. "Put this truck back on the road. We're going to the police station."

"Not until you put the gun down and listen to me. I don't want to hurt you."

Tension knotted her nerves, straining them until she thought she'd implode.

"But you will if you have to?" Staring into his eyes, she tried to find the truth. She was tired of running, tired of watching her back 24/7.

"Yes," he whispered.

It was true. She could see it in the determined set of his jaw, in the unwavering stare he focused on her. She swallowed, gauging the level of force he would no doubt use on her if given the chance. He was a tiger ready to pounce.

A trickle of fear dripped down her spine. "I've got no memory of you. Explain that."

"We spent one night together. The night before your overseas assignment with Borisov. I watched you climb into the limo from your bedroom window. Please look at the card."

Ava sucked in a deep breath. Had he been there? Had he really been there? Her memories were a ball of tangled thread. No two ends tied together, but she did remember that single moment. Looking up at her bedroom window. Climbing into the car. Was it enough to believe him?

She blinked.

In that instant he yanked the gun from her hand and tossed it onto the floorboard on the driver's side.

Panicked, she grabbed for the door handle, desperate to escape, but he was too quick.

Carson locked his arms around Ava before she could jump out of the pickup and run. He'd seen her panic flare with an intensity that threatened to push her over the edge.

Screaming, she fought him, but he held on to her.

"Ava! Stop. Think about the baby." Carson swallowed as she gave up the fight and settled against him. She was shaking as he loosened his grip.

What had happened to her after she got into the limo? The information *was* locked in her head.

"I'm taking you to Doc Resnick. Maybe he can help before we get on the military transport out of here at dawn."

"Please don't take me to McLean."

He tipped her chin up with his hand and stared down into her eyes. "You've been missing for four months. I can't help you if I don't know where you've been. You must have some kind of recall."

"Recall? I'll show you recall." She shrugged away from him and pulled up the sleeves of her blouse one after the other.

A wave of anger crushed him as he stared at her arms, bruised and dotted with needle marks.

He turned on the dome light, reached out and rotated her right arm, scanning her skin. "Defensive wounds, too. You put up one hell of a fight."

"Yeah. But did it do any good? I don't know who gave these to me." She shrank away from him. "I don't know what they did to me, my body, or my baby."

Rage circulated inside him, followed by concern. She'd been given drugs—the evidence was in plain sight. Had it affected her unborn child?

"I've got to get you to Doc Resnick."

"And what then?"

Carson slid back over into the driver's seat and recovered the gun from the floor-board, along with her business card.

"We make sure you're both okay."

"I'd like that." She looked over at him and he resisted the urge to touch her.

"Have you got a first-aid kit?" she asked.

"Yeah. In my pack."

"You're still bleeding. I'd like to patch you up."

"A peace offering?"

"For now." A slow smile spread on her lips.

He pulled out his backpack from under the seat and set it between them. Digging in to a side compartment, he pulled out the packet of gauze, antibiotic cream, alcohol preps and skin tape he always kept with him.

"It's not much." He handed it to her and slid his pack back down onto the floor. Inching closer, he raised his arms and pulled off his T-shirt to expose the injury.

Ava sucked in a breath, unable to explain the odd pounding of her heart. "Lift your arm."

He obeyed, raising his right arm and locking it behind his head.

She tried not to stare, tried not to make an idiot of herself, but her eyes were drawn to the taut lines of his chest highlighted in the dome light.

"Alcohol. I need some of that." Flustered, she opened the small plastic first-aid kit and took out three prepackaged preps.

She ripped them open with more gusto than she'd intended.

"You're going to enjoy this, aren't you?"

"No. But probably more than you."

Gingerly she reached toward him and brushed the wad of wipes over his wound.

He pulled in a sharp breath and let it out through pursed lips.

"The worst is over." She pulled her hand back without looking at him, sure he could see the color flaming in her cheeks.

Touching him turned her emotions inside out.

"This should soothe the burn." She cleaned her pinkie with an alcohol prep and squeezed out a generous amount of antibiotic cream onto her finger. Gently she smoothed it on his injury.

"You can fix me up anytime," he whispered against her ear as she placed a square of gauze over the wound.

His nearness drummed up desire in her body and she fought the crazy sensations that pounded out a sensual rhythm inside her.

"Hold that."

He pressed his hand over the bandage, catching her fingers before she could pull them away.

Heat raced up her arm and into her body. Her breath caught in her throat. She stared at him, mesmerized by the primal gleam in his eyes. She allowed her gaze to settle on his mouth before drawing it back up to his eyes.

A snippet of a memory bounced off her brain and she raced to catch it, snagging it just before she pulled her hand from underneath his.

Carson beat back his raging lust and pressed the piece of gauze down as hard as he could, letting the pain do battle with his out-of-control thoughts.

"Give me the tape," he said, holding out his hand.

Ava tore off a strip of skin tape and handed it to him.

One by one, he taped the edges of the bandage over his wound, rubbing it extra hard for good measure before he grabbed his T-shirt and put it back on.

"Thanks," he said as he pulled back out onto the Interstate, disgusted with himself for wanting her the way he did. She was his mission and he'd do well to remember that the next time he let his mind cross the line.

THE BALANCE OF THE DRIVE into the greater Seattle area was completed in silence. On several occasions he believed Ava was asleep, but then he'd feel her eyes on him in the shallow darkness.

It wasn't that he didn't believe her story. She had the physical scars to prove it. It was more of a caution. Was it possible she'd been turned by the Russians? Had she been able to give them top secret information during the four months she'd been MIA? And where the hell would she have gotten the information in the first place with her unclassified clearance level?

"I remembered something."

The whisper of her voice pulled Carson's focus from the road for an instant.

"A name." She straightened in the seat. "I

must have dozed off, because it was there when I woke up. Hinshaw."

"That's it?"

"Yeah."

"First or last?"

"I don't know. Probably last. I don't think I know anyone named Hinshaw, but then, I don't know what I know anymore."

Carson reached out and brushed her hand with his. Heat zapped up his arm and spread into his system. He pulled back, irritated with his body's overriding response to her.

"It's a start. My guess is, once the drugs are out of your system your head will begin to clear."

"And if it doesn't?"

"The psych department at McLean is your best bet."

Tension filled the air inside the cab of the pickup. "How do you know they're not to blame for the mental shape I'm in right now? How do you know they're not the ones who altered my memory in the first place?"

Carson considered her summation. She had a point. He was punching around in the dark and not making contact with anything solid.

"I don't. I'm going to reserve judgment until after you've had a chance to talk to Doc Resnick."

"Who is he?"

"Retired CIA. Ran the department at McLean for thirty years. I'd trust him with my life."

Apprehension coiled around Ava's body, pulling her nerves tight. She was at Agent Nash's mercy for the time being. Unarmed, and tired. Maybe he was right. Maybe seeing Dr. Resnick was the answer.

She tried to relax as he maneuvered the truck off the freeway and glanced in the rearview mirror.

"We've got company."

She reached for the armrest on the door, feeling the pickup accelerate as Carson turned right onto a four-lane highway.

Traffic was light. He changed lanes, pulled around a couple of cars and back into the outside lane.

She tried to relax as she looked in the side mirror, but the vehicle had followed their every move.

Her heart rate climbed. "You can't let them catch us."

Carson stepped down on the gas pedal, glad the old Ford had a souped-up motor under the hood.

Pulling into the left lane, he passed a slow-moving car and swung back into the right lane.

The car followed, picking up speed.

His nerves felt frayed. He made a hard right onto a two lane highway and gunned the engine.

He watched the speedometer climb past seventy.

The pursuing car dropped back, only visible on the tops of the rises approximately half a mile behind.

He maneuvered a sweeping left-hand corner and slammed on the brakes.

The pickup shuddered, its tires bouncing on the pavement in protest at the sudden deceleration.

Whipping the steering wheel hard to the right, he turned onto a narrow road and pulled down into the trees.

He killed the headlights and rolled to a stop.

Watching in the rearview mirror, he saw the chase car flash by.

"We ditched them for now." He put the truck in Reverse and backed out. His senses were heightened as he scanned the highway in both directions. They'd managed to lose the tail, but for how long?

A nagging suspicion took root in his brain.

He glanced at Ava. "You okay?"

"Yeah. My stomach's a little queasy, but I'll live."

"Doc lives in Tacoma. It's not far from here. We'll be there within the hour." He pulled back onto the highway and headed for the main road.

"And then what?"

"If we're lucky, we find out what happened to you in the last four months."

Ava tried to alleviate the dread infusing her body. She couldn't go back to CIA headquarters. She had to find a way to convince Carson of that fact...or she had to escape. Her life and the life of her unborn child depended on it. Maybe the doctor would come up with something. Maybe he'd be able to retrieve her lost memories. Maybe then Carson Nash would believe her.

CARSON SAT in the darkest corner of Dr. Gary Resnick's home office, listening to the coaxing notes of his voice as he took Ava deeper into hypnosis.

So far his attempts to unlock her secrets had failed. On a couple of occasions she'd even answered Gary's questions in Russian. An event that concerned him.

He rocked his head back and forth, trying to relieve the tension in his neck and between his shoulder blades. They were running out of time. The transport was scheduled to leave McChord AFB at 6:00 a.m. and he planned to be on it. Memories or no memories.

"On the count of three, you'll wake up. One, two, three."

She opened her eyes and leaned forward in the chair. "Please tell me you got something." There was desperation in her voice and Carson fought the urge to reassure her.

"I'm afraid not, but with drug therapy I might be able to get something."

Ava grimaced. "No. No drugs."

She stood up. "Is there any chance you have extra clothing. I need to shower and change."

Carson came to his feet. "There's no time."

"Please." She turned toward him, staring at him through eyes the color of deep-sea water. He relented. God only knew how long she'd been wearing the same clothes. A shower was a minor luxury.

"You're about the size of my daughter, Penny," Dr. Resnick said. "She's away at college. Her room is down the hall, second door on the left. I'm sure you can find something in there to wear. Take whatever you need."

"Thank you." She turned to leave the room.

"Fifteen minutes, max," Carson said to her back.

She nodded.

He watched her leave the room, but didn't speak until he heard a door close somewhere down the hallway.

"Level with me, Gary. What's going on in her head?"

"Memory modification, and or annihilation. It's an effective technique I pioneered and taught at McLean. Some of the interconnecting neuropathways in the brain are blocked, so she may remember, say, her address, but not her phone number. A childhood memory, but not what she ate for breakfast. The blocks I encountered in her are solid, but sometimes you can get minor recall by exposing the patient to familiar settings. The only other way through them is with drug interdiction."

"She's already been put through hell. There are at least a dozen needle marks in her arms."

"There's only one way to set blocks this solid. Traumatic stressors. They increase suggestibility. She may have witnessed a horrific event sometime after she went missing." Gary smoothed his hand over his head. "But her use of Russian concerns me the most. Have you considered she might be a double agent working for the Russians?"

Carson studied his friend in the dim light of the office. He'd considered it, all right. It would explain why they'd been holding her at the cabin, and it made sense that the CIA wanted her back in the fold. But for prosecution or counterintelligence measures, he wasn't sure. Then there was the NSA's involvement.

"My mission hasn't changed. I'm taking her to McLean. They can sort it out there."

"You could leave her with me. Let me try to get at the information."

Caution bunched Carson's nerves. "Negative. No more drugs." He hesitated. "She's pregnant, Gary."

Resnick blanched for an instant and pulled in an audible breath. "You're sure?"

"That's what she says. It's her body and I'm sure she knows what she's talking about."

"This could complicate the recovery process. It'll limit the range of drugs they can use on her." Gary Resnick stared at him, concern in his gray eyes. "She would be better off here."

Carson considered the offer for a moment. Considered the health of his unborn child. "Not necessary. I'll stay on once we get there. Make sure they take precautions for the baby as well as for her." He wasn't sure how Ava would take the news, but he'd already made up his mind.

Gary looked away. "Okay. But if there's any way I can help, you can call me anytime."

"Thanks." Carson extended his hand and they shook. "We've got to get going. Can't miss the transport."

"McChord Air Force Base?" Gary asked, turning back to his desk.

"Yeah."

"Good luck, then."

Carson nodded as Dr. Resnick sat down in his desk chair. "Where's your team?"

"Dark."

Gary nodded. "Chances are Ava's going to experience some violent headaches as she withdraws from the hypnotherapy drugs. Give her Tylenol."

"Okay. Thanks, Doc."

"You know the way out. Keep in touch."

Carson left the room, closing the door behind him.

An uneasy sensation traveled up his spine as he stopped at the bedroom door and raised his fist to knock, listening for movement behind the door. Nothing.

He grasped the knob, turned it and stepped into the room.

The lamp on the bedside table was on. Ava's crumpled blouse and pants lay in a heap on the floor, and next to them, his bulletproof vest.

An unexpected blaze of desire singed his nerves. He swallowed, determined to squash the longing in his body.

He'd crossed the line that night months ago, and he couldn't give free rein to his desires again.

Light shone from under the adjoining bathroom door. He moved toward it, listening to the sound of water running in the shower.

He knocked. "Ava. We've got to go."

No reply.

Carson attempted to turn the knob. The door was locked. He knocked again, harder this time. "Ava. Are you okay?"

Nothing.

He felt a wave of foreboding as he dug in to his pants pocket and pulled out his pocketknife. Opening the blade, he pushed it into the slot on the knob and gave it a turn.

The lock popped.

He pushed the door open.

Steam billowed out. The air was sauna-hot against his face.

Worried, he approached the bath and shoved back the shower curtain. The tub was empty.

Reaching down, he turned off the hot water faucet, his gaze settling on the open window above the toilet.

"Problem?" Gary asked from behind him.

"She's gone." Carson closed his knife and shoved it back into his pocket. "What's on the perimeter?"

"A wooded area."

"You search the house. I'm going outside to look for her. Be careful. She's unarmed, but she's not defenseless."

Carson moved past the doc, grabbing his vest on the way out of the bedroom. He pulled it on over his shirt and bolted down the hallway, out into the living room and out the front door. Drawing his 9 mm, he eased around the side of the house, letting his eyes adjust to the darkness.

He listened for movement.

Nothing.

Making out the back corner of the ranch-style home, he moved in next to the bathroom window she'd crawled out of. She had a ten-minute head start. How fast could she move? How far could she run?

A flash of admiration stilled his movements.

Ava Ross didn't want to go to McLean, and she was willing to risk injury to keep it from happening. Was there merit in her resistance?

Carson darted away from the protection of the house and moved into the woods, slipping in behind a tree.

Again he assessed his surroundings, listening for any indication that she shared the woods with him.

A slight breeze stirred in the tops of the trees, riffling the leaves. In the distance a dog barked. The odds were she'd hidden. Hunkered down close by to wait him out. Maybe she'd seen him move away from the house and made countermoves to avoid him.

They'd go in circles until time ran out and the transport left without them.

Determination pulsed inside him. He had a mission to complete.

Carson squatted, feeling around on the ground until he found a rock.

Aiming deep into the woods, he chucked it, hearing it cut through the air and smack into a tree well beyond his line of sight.

A muffled squeal came from the direction he'd thrown the stone.

Moving like a cat, he edged deeper into the trees, careful not to make a sound. The element of surprise would be his.

Shuffling footsteps froze him in his tracks. They'd come from the direction of the house, but Ava was in front of him—he was sure of it.

Had Dr. Resnick followed him?

Ava's scream slammed into his brain.

Carson lunged forward, following the sound.

Voices. There were voices up ahead.

He hit the dirt and crawled forward in the darkness intent on his target.

"Take it easy, Ross. You know what we want."

He held his breath, letting the words sink

into his brain. Dr. Resnick's summation regarding Ava's loyalties seemed to be proving out.

"I don't know what you're talking about. Let me go!" The desperation in her voice coiled his nerves. He couldn't let her be hurt, even if she'd turned.

The sound of Ava's cries drove him forward.

Carson came to his feet and burst into the clearing, gun raised.

One of the men held a flashlight beam directed on Ava's bare back, and the other man held a knife inches from her skin.

"Drop the knife," Carson demanded, staring at the men as they raised their eyes to meet his.

"This doesn't concern you." The man with the flashlight ground out the words.

"She concerns me." He scrutinized the two men wearing black.

They resembled the thugs they'd encountered back at the warehouse—probably CIA or NSA, but he wasn't sure.

"Who are you?" he asked, aware that neither man had followed his command, or shown any sign they intended to. "Let her go," he demanded.

Malice infused the air as Carson watched the man with the knife step back.

"Ava. Over here."

She jerked her arm free of the man's grasp and moved to Carson's side.

"You've got no idea what's going on. Stay out of it," one of the men warned.

"So fill me in." Carson braced for a fight. He didn't like the way the situation was shaping up. Reaching out, he steered her behind him.

In an instant the man who'd wielded the knife pulled a gun, but Carson beat him to the shot.

He squeezed off a round, hitting the man in the shoulder.

The thug stumbled backward and fell to the ground, cussing and sputtering.

His partner was next. He lunged forward, but Carson was ready. Raising his leg, he slammed his foot into the man's chest, sending him to the dirt next to his cohort.

He grabbed Ava's hand and whirled around. They ran through the darkness and out of the woods into Dr. Resnick's backyard.

Porch lights snapped on along the street. It wouldn't be long before the cops arrived. Gunshots in a residential neighborhood always got someone's attention.

By the time they made it to the truck parked a block away, the sound of sirens filled the night air.

Carson jerked open the driver's door and helped Ava in before climbing in next to her.

"Down!" He cupped her head with his hand, pushing her down in the seat.

A squad car rolled by, its lights flashing.

That was all he needed right now—to feed an explanation to the locals.

Carson rose up and peered over the dashboard.

The police unit stopped at the end of the block at the home next door to Dr. Resnick. He watched two officers climb out of the car and approach the house.

He waited until they went inside before he sat up and shoved the key into the ignition. The truck fired up.

Carson put it in Reverse and backed down

the street and around the corner before he flipped a U-turn and headed out of the area. He scanned the road from the rearview mirror to make sure they weren't being followed. The men who'd caught up with Ava in the woods didn't want a confrontation with the cops any more than he did. But one of them was going to need medical attention. Maybe that would slow them down.

"Are you okay?"

"Yeah."

"Are you going to tell me what you have that they want?" Anger fisted in his gut. He hated half-truths and disinformation.

"I don't know what they were talking about. All I've had for the last four months are the clothes on my back, until tonight."

Worry churned his thoughts as he turned on the headlights and pulled out onto the main road headed for McChord AFB. Whatever they wanted from her, they were willing to kill for it, and the sooner he knew what it was, the better their odds of surviving.

Chapter Five

Ava stared at the heap of scrambled eggs on her plate and back up at Carson, who sat across the long narrow table from her with an inquisitive gleam in his eyes.

When had she last eaten? She didn't know and it made her angry. Her unborn child needed sustenance as much as she did.

She picked up her fork and dug in, eating while worry filled her mind.

Carson Nash had claimed the baby she carried was his, but she couldn't be sure it wasn't a ruse designed to elicit her cooperation.

Glancing up between a bite and a sip of orange juice, she studied his face.

Was he her type? What *was* her type? Would she have allowed him into her bed?

Aggravated with her lack of recall, she polished off the eggs and chomped on her bacon. Maybe it didn't matter at this exact moment, but it was going to matter five months from now.

"You might want to…you've got some egg…" Carson made a wiping motion.

She picked up her napkin and brushed it across her chin. "Gone?"

"Yeah. Do you want more? We've got time."

"No, thanks."

A satisfied smile spread across his mouth, and a streak of desire rippled over her.

"I love a girl with an appetite and some meat on her bones."

She returned his grin, relaxing for the first time since she'd come to at the warehouse less than seven hours ago. She was safe with him. He'd already rescued her more than once. But there was still the matter of McLean. She couldn't go back there. And he was determined to return her.

She glanced around the almost empty hall. The base was a secure facility. The most she'd be able to do was hide. Maybe her chances were better at Andrews AFB, on her home turf. She pushed the plan back in her mind.

"Come on." Carson stood up. "We've got to get over to the flight deck and suit up. The transport leaves at 0600."

She stood and followed him around the perimeter of the mess hall, where he snagged a banana and a muffin from the chow line. "Put these in your pocket. You might need them on the flight."

She took the food.

Their fingers brushed in the handoff. A jolt of total awareness sang up her arm.

Ava looked into Carson's eyes, witnessing his moment of hesitation as he studied her. Was it the chemistry between them, or was he beginning to believe her fear of being returned to CIA headquarters was justified?

Maybe he was just working over the ways he planned to force her into the fold? She didn't know. She didn't want to know, because knowing would compel her to make a final decision about the character of the man who claimed to be her baby's father.

"Let's move." Carson turned and headed

out of the mess hall, confused by the jumble of emotions clouding his mind and his judgment.

The fire in her touch only made it worse, but he had a mission. One mission. To return Ava Ross to the CIA. So why couldn't he shake the idea that something was seriously wrong? In fact, the whole damn mission had an air of trouble about it that wouldn't dissipate. And there was the child she carried. His child. An innocent in the middle of it all.

A cauldron of protectiveness boiled over inside him, a need to shelter her and the baby from the harsh measures he knew he would have to take if she gave him any more trouble.

He would complete his mission.

They left the mess hall and tagged a ride to the flight deck hangar. The C-130 Hercules they were going to board sat on the tarmac being fueled and loaded.

Carson opened the door to the locker room and glanced inside. It was empty.

"You need to suit up." He guided Ava into the room and closed the door, moving to a closet, where he searched for a jumpsuit that would fit her.

"It's orders. You can't look like a civilian—not even on a transport."

She stood behind him with her arms crossed. "Grab me a small."

"Got it." Carson pulled out a small flight suit in olive-green and handed it to her. "There's a women's section around the corner."

"Thanks." She took the uniform and went in search of privacy.

Carson felt wary as he pulled out a flight suit for himself and closed the closet. He didn't trust Ava. She'd tried to skip out on him at the doc's place, but she'd be a fool to think she could do it here. Still, he couldn't help but worry.

A curtain separated the men's section from the women's, and he took up a spot on the bench closest to the doorway.

Bending over, he stared under the curtain, scanning for her legs. She'd chosen a bench close to the divider. He relaxed as he stared at her feet. There was only one way out of the room. She'd have to come through him if she tried to pull another escape attempt.

Stripping down to his boxers, Carson

shoved his legs into the flight suit, pulled it on and zipped up the front. Sitting down again, he pulled his boots back on and started to lace them, but he couldn't resist taking another peek at Ava.

He glanced under the curtain where her legs were visible from the knee down. His gaze locked on the bruises covering both of her calves.

Anger roared to life inside him. "Grab something and cover up. I'm coming in." He stood up.

Ava let out a yelp of protest, but it didn't deter him. He pushed aside the curtain and stepped toward her.

"Why didn't you tell me you were injured?"

A look of defiance crossed her face. "I'm on the mend."

"Sit!" he demanded, glad when she followed orders and sat down on the bench, clutching the flight suit to her body.

Reaching out, he grasped her right ankle in his hands.

A muffled cry escaped her lips before he looked up, witnessing a grimace of pain on her face.

"You should have said something."

"It was healing, until those thugs grabbed me in the woods last night. I kicked one of them and aggravated it."

"So the first time you injured it was also kicking someone?"

"I don't know for sure, but yeah, it's a defensive move."

"It could be sprained." Carson felt all along her leg from the knee down, ending at her foot. "You need an X-ray. It's the only way to know for sure." He looked up and saw her face brighten with anticipation for an instant before she hid her expression.

She was looking for another chance to escape, and a busy hospital would do it.

He gritted his teeth. "It's going to have to wait until we get to Andrews. They can patch you up there at the base. For now, I'll wrap it."

The excitement faded from her eyes, confirming his suspicion. Agent Ava Ross was still looking for a way out in spite of the danger on their trail.

On a gut level he tuned in to her fear. She'd put up one hell of a fight somewhere along the way, and the injuries to her body proved it.

He stared at her ankle for a moment, noting the color of the bruises. The ones from earlier were purple…fresh, but the coloring farther up her shin above the ankle had turned yellow and green, signs of an old injury.

Heat circled in his veins as he recalled her legs four months ago. Long, silky, void of trauma and entangled with his.

He stood up. "Get dressed. I'll pull the first aid kit and an ice pack. It'll keep the swelling down until we get you to a doctor."

Ava stared after Carson as he disappeared through the curtain, disappointed that her brief chance at another escape had been shot down. Her ankle hurt like the devil. She could still use it, still maneuver. But the feel of his hands on her had confirmed one thing for certain.

Physical contact between them *always* generated sparks.

She pulled the flight suit from around her midsection and gave it a shake before sliding both her legs into the uniform. She'd feel more comfortable dressed the next time she faced Carson Nash. It wasn't that she hadn't enjoyed the contact. It was the fact that she didn't want to feel anything for him when she took the measures she planned to take.

Carson squeezed the ice pack until he felt the vial inside pop and start the chemical reaction. It got cold in his hand as he headed for the locker room.

Maybe he was being too harsh with her, making her wait for medical treatment, but he knew what he'd seen in her eyes was trouble.

Trouble that could endanger them both if he ever let her get away.

Carson stepped through the curtain and stopped.

The bench was empty. His senses went into overdrive.

"Ava!" He turned around, but not fast enough.

Crack! She caught him on the back of the head with a hard object.

His vision blurred for an instant before he reacted.

Whirling around, he dropped the Ace bandage and the ice pack and lunged for her, catching her with the broomstick in the air ready to take another whack at his head.

He locked his arms around her, pushing her backward until she hit the wall.

The weapon clattered to the floor as he pinned her raised arms over her head. "What are you doing? I don't want to hurt you, but you have to stop this."

He stared down into her watery green eyes, wide with panic. She shuddered.

Slowly he released her arms, but he continued to press her against the wall with his body, determined to come to an understanding.

"I'm not going to let you go until you promise to behave."

She stared up at him. The panicked expression was gone, but he could still see determination in her eyes, mixed with mistrust and desperation, like an animal trapped in a cage, looking for a way out.

"Why don't you believe me? Why won't you help me?" Her voice wavered.

"My mission is to deliver you to the CIA. Period."

"Even if I know what they'll do to me?"

"You've been compromised. They only want to debrief you. They wouldn't have sent me or my team in to rescue you if they planned to hurt you. They'd have done it in the field."

"What if you're wrong? What if you've been played and they're responsible for everything that's happened?"

Carson swallowed as he considered his gut reactions from the moment he'd pulled the black hood off her head and discovered someone he'd thought was dead.

For an instant he wanted to believe her, but other than the defensive marks on her body and the attempts on her life, he had no proof.

"You're hurting me," she whispered.

Slowly he stepped back, reluctant to turn her loose. The points of his body where they'd made physical contact buzzed with sensation.

He rubbed the back of his head, feeling the knot left by the broom handle. Holding his stance, he stared at her. "You don't know where those injuries came from. If you could remember some of what took place and where…I'd be more likely to believe you."

She clenched her teeth and he instinctively braced for another attack, but it didn't come.

"You know I can't do that. Dr. Resnick couldn't even pull anything out of me."

"Then McLean is your best hope."

She glared at him and attempted to move around him, but he snagged her arm. "Not this time, sweetheart. From here on out we're joined at the hip. Now, sit down and let me bandage your ankle. Our ride out of here is ready to taxi."

Obediently she sat down as Carson scooped up the bandage and the ice pack.

Ava hiked up the pant leg on her flight suit and stared at the wall in front of her rather than at him. She tried to ignore the feel of his hands as he carefully wrapped the bandage around her foot, ankle and halfway up her shin, but the gentleness in his touch sent shivers through her body that she couldn't ignore. He finished and tucked the loose end back down into the bandage. "That should do it. You can put the ice pack on your ankle once we take off. Is it too tight?"

She stared down at him. Heat crept into her cheeks as a wave of desire crashed on her nerves. "It's good."

He slid her service flats onto her feet. "Where are your clothes?"

She pointed to the jeans and T-shirt rolled up on the bench.

Carson snagged them and shoved them into his pack. "Let's get moving." He helped her stand and put his arm around her waist. "Those C-130 pilots are a punctual bunch. They won't wait for long."

Leaning into him, she let him help her aboard the waiting aircraft through the rear cargo door.

"Good morning, sir," a baby-faced crewman greeted them as they moved into the belly of the plane. "If you'll come with me, I'll show you to your seats."

"I thought this flight was supposed to be an empty return." Carson nodded to the Humvee parked in the belly of the otherwise empty aircraft and loaded down with cargo parachutes.

"Oh. The Hummer. It's a last-minute drop at Fort Belvoir Military Reservation in Virginia. It'll add half an hour to our flight time."

"It's going out on a chute?" Carson asked as they followed the flight-suit-clad young man.

"Yes, sir."

"No problem. We've got plenty of time to meet our deadline."

"Here you go." The crewman pointed at a pair of jump seats near the front of the aircraft.

"Thanks. How many crew onboard today?" Carson pulled off his pack and pushed down one of the jump seats.

"Three, including myself, and I wouldn't be here if this vehicle could push the deployment button itself."

He gave the young man a nod before helping Ava into the seat. Kneeling in front of her, he put the large ice pack on her ankle and tied it in place. "It should last for three to four hours."

She nodded and reached for her shoulder harness belt.

Carson helped her into the safety setup and strapped himself in while the crewman closed the airplane's massive rear cargo door.

He handed her a pair of headphones, as much for communication as for ear protection. She put them on and adjusted the mouthpiece. He did the same.

One by one the engines whined and came to life, until the aircraft rumbled like a freight train and lurched forward.

"Ever been on one of these tuna boats?" he asked.

"I don't know. Not that I remember." She looked over at him and grinned.

Her response made him smile and he tried to relax. They were finally rolling. They'd be on the ground again by late afternoon. She'd be delivered to CIA headquarters shortly after that, so why didn't the information sit well in his gut?

"If you want me to come into the fold with you, I will." He turned toward her, witnessing her look of confusion.

"Say again," she said into the mouthpiece.

"I'm coming in with you. Make sure you're treated right." He stared into her face, hoping for some kind of acceptance. Her fate was, after all, sealed. Sealed in the belly of a C-130. There was no way out until they landed at Andrews AFB outside Washington, D.C., in six and a half hours. He could make peace with his doubts by then. Maybe tagging along was the only way to do that. The only way to assure that Ava and his child weren't harmed.

"Okay." She nodded and looked away.

Ava tried to calm the fear in her stomach with the knowledge that Carson was going to come in with her, but it did little to alleviate her concern.

He was an agent. An IAops agent. The kind the CIA would deny existed. Perhaps she should consider herself lucky it was him next to her and not a suit.

Maybe there was still time to convince him McLean was a bad idea. If not, there was always escape.

THE CONSTANT DRONE of the aircraft engines lulled Carson into complacency. He looked at his watch. One hour until touchdown at Andrews.

He glanced over at Ava, sound asleep in her seat. Taking the liberty, he let his gaze slide down her body and found himself staring at her abdomen.

He could just make out the small round bulge below her navel, covered by the taut flight suit. He resisted the urge to cover the bump with his hand. To feel the hard evidence under his palm.

"Sir."

Carson started, looking up at the young crewman who stood in front of him. "Yeah."

"The captain would like to speak with you."

Warning rose in his gut. He tamped it down, unfastened his harness and stood up, letting the blood flow return to his legs.

He followed the crewman to the three-stair platform up into the cockpit of the aircraft. He climbed the steps, opened the door and went inside.

The captain of the airplane looked up from his seat at the flight controls. "Close the door," he said, before extending his hand.

Carson pulled the door shut and reached

out, shaking the pilot's hand. "Agent Carson Nash."

"I'm Captain Springer Davis. This is my cocaptain, Ray White."

"Your crewman said you needed to speak with me."

"We just received a direct transmission from Andrews base command. We've been ordered to remand your prisoner, Agent Ava Ross, upon arrival."

Suspicion battered Carson's senses, but he kept his cool. "Any word on the order's origin?"

"Negative. I just fly the plane."

"Are we on schedule?"

"Affirmative. Down to the minute."

Carson reached for the door handle. "She's all yours once we're on the ground."

The captain nodded.

Carson left the cockpit, taking the stairs at a leisurely pace he didn't feel. Something was wrong. Dead wrong.

He glanced around for the crewman and spotted him in his seat on the other side of the cockpit door. Slipping back into his seat, he closed his eyes and leaned his head back against the headrest, letting his mind work the details his gut had already deciphered.

Ava's claims might be true, but without a name to go with the redirect order, he didn't have anything to go on.

He couldn't let her be taken from his custody until he knew she'd be safe—and if that meant evasion, then so be it.

Carson opened his eyes and looked at his watch. They were twenty minutes from the drop zone. He gazed at the Hummer sitting in the belly of the plane and made his decision.

He stood up, making his way over to the crewman's seat. "Hey, I can't sit any longer. Can I help you prepare this beast for launch?"

"Sure." The airman glanced at his watch. "It's about that time anyway." He stood up and moved toward the Hummer. "Pull the tie-downs on the corners. Make sure they're unhooked and clear of the roll-out track."

"You got it." Carson moved down the left side of the Humvee, releasing the tie-down straps one by one. Stepping up, he looked inside the vehicle. The keys swung from the ignition. Reaching out, he tried the door latch. It opened in his hand, just as the crewman came around the tail end of the Hummer.

"Better close that tight," he said, pulling the last tie-down strap free.

Carson shut the door. "What's next?" he asked, his hands on his hips.

"The captain comes over the intercom, tells me we're over the drop zone and lowers the cargo door. I tether off and punch that red extrication button over there." He indicated a button near the cockpit door. "And it's bye-bye baby, off into the wild blue."

"Sounds simple enough. Does the captain close the hatch?"

"Yeah. After the cargo launch sensor light goes out."

"Smooth operation. Thanks for the rundown."

"You better buckle up. When the door drops, the wind currents can be rough. Men have been sucked out of the plane." The crewman turned around.

In one swift move Carson put him in a choke hold and pulled off his headphones.

The crewman went limp in his arms.

Carson dragged him over to his seat and buckled him in. Grabbing a tie-down strap, he bound the man's hands together in front of him.

There was no need to gag the crewman, he decided, doubting anything could be heard over the drone of the aircraft engines.

He rushed to the seat where Ava still slept, and pulled off her headphones.

She startled, her eyes flew open and she stared up at him as if he'd lost his mind. He put his hand over her mouth and pointed at the Hummer. "I believe you," he mouthed, watching her absorb the information. "Let's go."

He undid the seat-belt buckle and pulled her up, feeling her resist. "It's the only way. They want to take custody of you at Andrews."

Her features softened, her shoulders straightened. She nodded.

He pointed at the Hummer. "Get in!"

Ava couldn't believe what was happening. One moment she'd been lost in sleep, the next she was preparing to climb into a Hummer for a ride out of the sky.

Her legs shook as she wobbled to the driver's door of the vehicle.

Carson pulled open the door and she climbed inside.

"Roll down the window, put on the emergency brake and pop it out of gear."

She obeyed, cranking the handle until the window disappeared. She yanked on the emergency brake and pulled the Hummer out of gear.

"Get in the passenger seat and buckle up! It's going to be a rough ride."

An instant of terror struck her, but she forced it back. She slid into the passenger seat and buckled up.

Carson grabbed his pack and pushed it through the driver's window just as the captain's voice came over the loudspeaker.

"We're over the drop zone. Door down." A hazard warning buzzed three times. The massive cargo door mechanically unlatched and began to drop.

Ava put her hands over her ears. The noise level inside the belly of the plane intensified. Why wasn't Carson in the Hummer with her?

Panic streamed over her, turning into a torrent as she watched him approach the cockpit door.

Was he crazy? He should be strapping in right now, but he was just standing there staring at her.

"You're clear to launch," the captain said over the roar of the wind.

She watched Carson punch a red button and felt the Hummer jolt backward on the launch tracks.

Terror sliced through her as he lunged toward the moving vehicle, fighting the air currents swirling around him.

He rounded the front bumper and dragged himself along the side of the vehicle.

"Hurry!" Ava yelled, glancing in the side mirror at the clear blue sky five feet behind the rolling Humvee.

If he didn't get inside before the rear wheels left the platform, he'd be sucked out of the aircraft.

Ava's heart hammered in her chest.

Carson jumped onto the step rail.

Thump. The rear wheels dropped off the back of the cargo gate.

She closed her eyes and waited for the nightmare to end. Carson Nash was as good as dead.

Chapter Six

With all the strength he could muster, Carson dived through the open window of the Hummer, grabbed the seat belt and wrapped it around his hand.

In slow motion the vehicle dropped out of the belly of the airplane.

Carson held his breath, feeling the Humvee rock back and go vertical.

The auto deployment cord hissed in the wind.

He braced for the jolt, hanging on for dear life.

The parachutes snapped, filling with air.

Bobbing like a yo-yo at the end of its string, the Hummer jerked.

Carson's teeth rattled in his head.

Free fall ceased, and they settled into a swaying glide to earth.

He pulled himself the rest of the way through the window, and up into the driver's seat, where he buckled in.

Only then did he look over at Ava.

Her eyes were closed, her skin ashen.

Reaching out, he touched her.

She opened her eyes, staring at him in disbelief, before poking him with her finger.

"Made it."

She nodded, a wry smile spreading on her lips. "I wasn't sure."

"I wondered, too." He rolled up the window, cutting down on the noise level inside the Hummer as it dropped slowly to earth, buoyed by three massive parachutes.

"In half an hour, they'll discover we decided to take another flight." Carson stared out the front windshield at the C-130 cargo plane growing smaller and smaller on the horizon.

"They'll radio Belvoir's control tower, where they'll dispatch an MP unit to scour the drop zone for us."

"What?" Ava asked, an edge of fear in her voice.

"That's why we have to drive this rig." He searched the ground, trying to pinpoint the location they'd most likely land. He spotted an open area with a road through the middle of it. There were trees within half a mile in both directions. "If we can make it to the trees, we'll change into civilian clothes. From there, we'll pick up the road and hope to hell we can get a ride. Otherwise we're going to have to lie low until nightfall."

Looking down at the circumference of the drop zone, he searched for the equipment recovery team, but the landscape was clear. With any luck they'd be able to make the dash undetected.

He guessed their drop time was less than two minutes out. "When we hit dirt, we might bounce. Lean forward and put your arms and hands over your head, brace until we come to a complete stop. Do you understand?" He looked over at her.

She nodded.

"Good." Reaching into the back of the Hummer, he pulled his pack up into the seat next to him. "Can you run on your ankle?"

"I'm sure going to try."

He looked at the tree line some three hundred yards from the drop zone. Staring hard, he gauged the wind direction. The tops of the trees were blowing due east.

Reaching down, he released the emergency brake and wobbled the gearshift to make sure the rig was in neutral.

He put the wind speed at approximately ten mph. Not great, but if his plan worked, they'd pick up half the distance.

In his peripheral vision he caught a flash of movement on the ground. Straining to look over his shoulder, he spotted a dust trail. Following to the source, he saw a single vehicle approximately three miles from the drop zone.

"You have to get out of your seat belt the instant we touch the ground."

"Okay."

"The pickup crew is going to be right behind us."

An instant of fear widened her eyes.

"Don't panic—we're going to make it."

She swallowed and assumed the brace position.

Carson kept his head up and turned the

Hummer's key to the start position, unlocking the steering column. At the last second before they hit the ground, he assumed the brace position.

The Hummer landed, bounced forward and continued to roll across the open field.

Carson rose up and grabbed the steering wheel, aiming for the grove of trees three hundred yards east. He could hear the wind crack in the massive parachutes overhead. "Hang on."

Steering with the pitch of the wind, he let their sail do the work until the Hummer gradually began to slow, and rolled to a stop.

The green canopy settled over them, enclosing the vehicle in a drab olive shroud.

"Let's move!" Carson popped his seat belt, pulled on the emergency brake, grabbed his backpack and climbed out of the driver's door.

They'd ridden an extra 150 yards, courtesy of the wind. And they were going to need every extra second it provided.

Ava's heart was beating so hard she could hear it in her eardrums. She undid her seat belt and scampered over the console into the driver's seat. The cover of green had a disorienting effect on her senses, but she kept her eyes on Carson and climbed out the driver's door.

He gave it a kick shut and took her hand, shoving through the yards and yards of parachute silk that hid them from the world outside.

They made the edge of the chute and Carson lifted it slowly. The sun blinded Ava for an instant.

"Our target is those trees."

She stared at the grove of maples, wishing they were closer. "Okay. I can do this." She gathered her nerve.

"Go!" Carson yelled, bolting forward with her hand in his. He didn't dare look over his shoulder. The pickup team would be on the drop zone soon. He just hoped it wasn't soon enough to catch sight of the stowaways who'd dropped from the sky along with the vehicle.

Ava pushed forward, fighting the fatigue in her body. She focused on the tree line and regulated her breathing, feeling a surge of energy. She didn't know if it was Carson's constant hold on her hand or the fact that she'd eaten well this morning and slept on the aircraft.

The field was covered in tall grass that hit her midthigh. The ground under her feet was flat, but she could feel the slight decline as they moved closer to the tree line and cover.

Her foot lodged in a chuckhole before she could avoid it. Intense pain shot through her ankle and radiated into her leg.

A shriek squeezed from between her lips as she launched forward headed for the dirt.

Only Carson's grip on her kept her from landing hard. He eased her down into the grass and went down on his belly beside her.

He raised his finger to his lips.

Ava wanted to cry out. The pain was intense. Her injured ankle pounded and throbbed.

But the sound of the approaching vehicle stilled her.

Clamping her teeth together, she closed her eyes to wait for the inevitable.

Carson listened intently to the squeal of brakes as the pickup team rolled up on the parachute-covered Humvee and stopped.

They'd managed to make it fifty yards before Ava's ankle had given out. He glanced over at her now, lying next to him on her back. Her eyes were closed, but he could see the amount of pain she was in. Her teeth were clamped shut, her jaw, rigid, a hand protecting her belly.

Sympathy laced through him, the weight of her suffering catching in his brain. He needed to get her to a doctor ASAP.

The sound of voices drew his attention, and he focused on the words he could decipher.

"Fuel…roll the chutes…ice pack."

Carson listened for any change in the crew's level of concern. He should have made sure Ava still had her ice pack, but he'd neglected to check. He'd disobeyed the team's cardinal rule. In clean, out clean.

A curse rested on his tongue as he waited…hoping the crewmen would let it go.

The rise and fall of their voices gave no indication they were concerned about the ice pack lying in the floor of the Humvee. It was only going to make sense when the pilot of the C-130 radioed Belvoir's central command and let them know they'd inadvertently dropped off more than an empty vehicle. Carson listened to yards of parachute silk skim across the grass before he heard the clank of a gas tank lid rattling loose, and the sound of fuel gurgling into the rig.

They'd be on their way soon. Worried, he glanced over at Ava. With her ankle possibly broken, they'd play hell moving any faster than a couple of turtles in a snowstorm.

They needed transportation.

"Do you think you can belly crawl to the tree line?" He looked over at her and watched her eyes flicker open.

"Do I have to?"

"If you don't want to wait for nightfall and a miserable hike out of here on that ankle."

She raised herself up on her elbows and looked down at her feet. Carson couldn't help but stare at the tiny bulge in her abdomen. He swallowed against a zap of worry and refocused on her face. "I want you to crawl into the brush and change into your street clothes. I'm going to do the same."

"Okay." She glanced over at him and he watched courage gather in her demeanor.

"I'm going to come running out of the grove, waving my arms. They're going to stop me and I'm going to make some outrageous claims. Go with it."

"All the way."

"Let's move. We don't have much time." He turned onto his belly and moved through the grass with Ava not far behind. Still listening to the movements of the crew, they reached the tree line and paused. The landscape sloped off gradually, leaving them a secure spot just below the lip of a slight ravine.

Carson sat up and pulled off his pack. Digging into it, he pulled out Ava's clothes along with his own.

She flinched as he slid down the zipper on his flight suit, and she turned away, grabbing her own clothes from the pile.

The sound of her zipper gave him pause as he wriggled his shoulders out of the fabric and pulled on his T-shirt.

The sight of Ava's bare back put fire in his veins and he recalled the feel of her skin under his lips.

"Dammit," he whispered under his breath as he refocused his energy on getting dressed, instead of lusting after her. He needed to keep his head in the game.

She pulled on her blouse and he stared at her back, remembering how he'd caught the men holding her in the woods. They'd had her shirt up, her back exposed.

He pulled on his pants. It was significant, but why?

"I'm going to take off. You've got less than two minutes to finish dressing and stuff the flight suits into my backpack." He reached in and pulled out a camera before looping the strap over his head. "Be ready."

"I will." She stared up at him. He was taken by the look of sheer determination on her face. She'd been a good agent. She'd received commendation for superior service. Somewhere in that brain of hers were the answers that were going to save her life, and maybe his. He just had to hang tough until he found them.

Standing up, he lurched forward at a run. "Help. Somebody please help." With one hand, Carson held the camera to keep it from bouncing as he ran, and with the other he waved at the stunned crew staring at him as if he'd lost his mind.

"Help." He ran straight for them, judging their reactions as he moved in closer and finally stopped just short of the Humvee.

"My wife's been injured. She's right over there. Can you help us?"

"Slow down, sir. Are you aware this is a restricted area?"

"Restricted? From what?"

"Civilians."

"No way. We were on Telegraph Road. There weren't any signs."

"What are you doing here, sir?" The senior officer stepped forward and Carson sized him up.

"We were bird-watching. I spotted a yellow-rumped warbler. He's too far east. I had to stop and try to get a shot." He deliberately raised his camera to add validity to the story. "But he took off. We gave chase. My wife stepped in a hole and fell. I'm sure she needs medical assistance. If we could just get a ride back to the main road, we'll be out of your hair."

Carson braced for a positive answer. The alternative wasn't pleasant, and it might draw attention along with a detail of armed soldiers, which he wasn't prepared to battle at the moment.

The senior officer glanced over at his second in command, then back at Carson. "Where's your wife?"

"At the edge of the tree line...she's pregnant with our first child."

He saw the senior officer pause. "How far along?"

"Just four months, but I'm worried."

The officer was already moving past him, and he jogged up beside him. "I hope this doesn't cause any trouble. I mean, we never intended to enter a restricted area. And it's a damn good thing you guys were here, because my wife could be in bad shape."

"Take it easy, man. My wife just gave birth to our first child. We'll get you out to the main road."

"Thank you." Carson slowed a bit, catching

his breath. The ruse was almost a done deal. If Ava did her part, they'd be in the clear.

"Over here." They paused on the edge of the shallow ravine and Carson located Ava sitting in the grass where he'd left her. She was dressed in civilian clothes, the stuffed backpack on the ground next to her.

"She loves to bird-watch with me. We try to get out every couple of weeks. Last week we discovered a black-billed cuckoo over in Maryland." Carson prayed Ava had been listening to his spiel. They closed in on her and he watched her try to stand up. She made it up onto her feet just as he moved in next to her and put his arm around her waist for support.

"He's in that tree, Drake. If you hurry you might get the shot."

Carson smiled at her, warmed by her acting abilities as much as the feel of her body next to his. "Always the zealous one, aren't you dear? But the warbler will have to wait. These officers are going to give us a ride to the main road."

She looked at the two officers and smiled

sweetly. "Oh, thank you. I'm not sure I could have gotten very far on this ankle."

"You're welcome, miss, but we'd better get moving before command gets perturbed. Officer Gracowski, take a hike and bring the Humvee over. I'll follow in the jeep."

"Yes, sir." The officer turned, quickly covered the distance to the vehicles, climbed in and fired up the engine.

In a matter of minutes, Carson and Ava were seated in the Hummer they'd ridden to the ground and were being driven to the main road.

Carson tried to relax as he mentally went over the layout of the military reservation.

"There's a pullout on the northeast corner about a mile from here. That's where our car is parked."

"You hiked a hell of a long way."

"Anything for a snapshot of that bird." Carson expelled a chuckle he didn't feel and watched the officer smile. "Do we need to fill out a report or something…I mean, we're not in trouble, are we?"

"Not today. The captain didn't see fit to run you in."

"Thank goodness," Ava said in a grateful tone.

"But I wouldn't be caught out here again," the officer warned.

"No problem. We plan to steer clear of this place."

"Here we are." He applied the brake and came to a stop next to an expansive pullout in the road.

Carson hoped he'd been right in his recall of the place.

Sure enough, five vehicles sat in the lot at various angles. "There's our car." Carson focused on a gray sedan, not because it was the best-looking rig in the pullout, but because it was the one he figured he could hot-wire the fastest.

"Do you need help?" the officer offered.

"No, thanks. We can take it from here. Thanks for the ride." He helped Ava out of the Hummer and closed the door, waving to the officer.

He put his arm around her. "Don't turn around," he whispered as he led her to the car.

Listening, he heard the Hummer pull

away. Still moving toward the car, he didn't hesitate until he heard the rig shift into second gear, knowing the officer had pulled out onto the main road and would soon be out of sight.

"How did you know there would be cars here?"

"I didn't. But there's a pond to the north-east. I've been there more than a couple of times. I just hoped there would be someone here with a fishing pole and catfish on the brain."

Carson stopped next to the car and scanned the surrounding area, shadowed by oak, maple and river willow. The fishing hole was less than an eighth of a mile away. He scoped out the trail leading down a steep hill before it disappeared into the grove of trees. He could just make out a couple of fisherman through the dense growth.

"Wait here." He left Ava at the rear of the car and walked around to the front. Placing his hand on the hood of the vehicle, he felt for engine heat.

It was stone cold.

He moved back toward her and took a

glance inside the car. He stopped and pulled the latch on the driver's door; it opened in his hand.

"We're out of here, sweetheart. Take the lookout point."

Ava shuffled forward, using the car as a crutch until she reached the front of the vehicle. Staring down toward the pond, obscured by foliage, she focused on the trail—the line of ascent that could lead to disaster.

The sharp pain in her ankle had died to a dull throb. She was grateful, but she knew it could flare again if she pushed too hard.

In the background she could hear Carson behind the steering wheel of the car as he ripped into the steering column.

Her heart rate picked up. She tried to relax by pulling in several deep breaths of the early-evening air, but it only made her feel dizzy.

She leaned against the hood of the car to steady herself. An odd sensation akin to butterflies churned in her abdomen. Ava swallowed against a flood of emotion and concentrated on the feeling. Movement, deep inside her body.

Her child.

Tears burned behind her eyelids as the realization hit her. In that instant her baby was no longer a bit of knowledge, but a viable factor in her life.

Turning, she sought out Carson, only to see that his head was bent as he worked on their ride.

Movement caught her attention. She turned back and refocused on the pathway.

A fisherman clad in a red T-shirt came out of the trees next to the pond and shuffled onto the trail.

"Someone's coming," she said in as even a voice as she could generate. Glancing over her shoulder, she saw Carson look up.

The car's engine roared to life with a loud rumble and a puff of gray-blue smoke.

Looking back down the trail, she saw the fisherman's head come up.

Panic rocked her body.

"Oh, damn!"

"Hey!" the fisherman bellowed, dropping his gear in a heap and breaking into a run. "That's my car!"

Chapter Seven

Ava scrambled around the hood of the sedan and made for the passenger door, her heart in her throat.

She slid into the seat wishing the car had wings instead of wheels.

Carson sat up and slammed the door, put the car in Reverse and stepped on the gas pedal.

The car shot backward in a cloud of dust and gravel.

Spinning the steering wheel, he aimed for the exit and glanced in the rearview mirror as the angry car owner charged into the parking lot.

"I hope he forgot his cell phone today," Carson said as he whipped out of the pullout and took a right. "We've got ten minutes before the cops are all over us. We've got to ditch this car."

"But we just took it."

"We can't outrun a radio transmission." Carson raced down Telegraph Road, braked and took a hard left onto Hayfield. "I'm heading for a population center. We'll be harder to locate there."

He glanced at Ava. Her cheeks were void of color, her skin blanched.

"You okay?"

"Yeah. Just a little too much excitement. I'll be fine."

She would be fine and he planned to make sure of it, just as soon as he could. "Springfield Mall. We'll ditch the car there." Braking, he came to a stop and took a right onto Beulah Road. In less than a minute he reached the shortcut up to Franconia. He veered left and gunned the engine.

Through the trees he could see the mall complex spread out over a massive area.

Carson slowed and turned left on the 613. He was relaxed by the time he turned into the mall parking lot and parked the car.

He pulled the ignition wires apart, and

the engine died. Reaching into his pocket, he took out two pieces of cloth. "Wipe off anything you touched."

Ava nodded and took the fabric, rubbing it on the seat-belt release, the seat and the dashboard where she'd put her hands in a moment of panic. Reaching out, she opened the car door and climbed out before wiping down the inside door handle.

Carson followed suit, working his rag over every possible nook and cranny. Not that it mattered. His fingerprints didn't exist in any database, but they needed to make a clean break, considering the car's owner might have seen Ava, and might be able to describe her to the police. They couldn't risk leaving any clues behind.

He shoved the rag into his pocket and came around the car to the passenger side.

"Our ride out of here isn't too far away." He put his arm around Ava's waist and directed her toward an area crowded with people waiting for the bus.

He felt calmer as they merged into the back of the line. "How's the ankle?"

"I think I can walk on it." She stepped away from him.

Suddenly and regrettably, he missed the feel of her. Looking over at her, he admired her grit for an instant.

"Here it comes," she said.

He followed her gaze and watched the city bus turn on its flashers and grind to a stop. Taking one last look over his shoulder, he caught sight of a black sedan moving slowly into the parking lot. It turned into a space not far from where they'd left a car.

He put his hand on the small of Ava's back, moving her deeper into the crowd of people waiting their turn to board the bus.

Two men climbed out of the car.

Carson's gut twisted as he watched them move in on the abandoned car and casually look inside. How the hell had they found the car so fast? Unless...

Anger burned through him as he considered the only possibility.

His gaze locked on Ava. They'd been pursued from the moment he'd laid eyes on her at the cabin in Washington State.

They stepped into the stairwell of the bus

and climbed on board, then he motioned to a seat on the opposite aisle and let her slide in first. From his vantage point inside the bus, he watched the two men move away from the car. One kept glancing down at some sort of gadget in his hand as he turned from side to side.

Carson's stomach clenched. They were being tracked. And not with good old-fashioned footwork, but with a GPS of some sort.

The last passenger climbed aboard and the driver closed the doors.

The two men looked up in the direction of the bus.

Worry shot through him. They'd be in their car and in hot pursuit in a matter of minutes.

Casually Carson draped his arm around Ava's shoulders and pulled her next to his body. At first she resisted, but he smiled over at her and she loosened up.

Leaning close, he whispered in her ear, "You've got a bug. Care to tell me where you're hiding it?"

She turned on him, her eyes widening in

disbelief. Was it because he'd figured it out? Or was the information really news to her? He couldn't be sure.

"A couple of thugs pulled into the parking lot not far behind us. By now they're probably splitting traffic to catch up. You'd better come clean before the next stop."

Reaching out, he smoothed a lock of hair out of her face and tucked it behind her ear, a move that looked and felt intimate to him, even if he'd used it only to puff up the ruse in the eyes of the passengers sitting around them.

"If you don't, I'll search you."

Ava couldn't believe what he'd threatened to do. She jerked back and stared into his intense blue eyes. They were hard as steel and dancing with malice.

Carson Nash was 100-percent serious.

Her heart thundered in her chest. "Don't you think I'd know if I'd been tagged?"

His gaze never wavered as he continued to stare at her. The mistrust she could see in his eyes shattered her fragile sense of security.

She was his mission. Nothing more. But then, why had he confessed to being the father of her unborn child rather than just dragging her into the fold kicking and screaming?

"Go ahead. Search me."

An instant of anticipation flared in his eyes. A slow, devil-may-care smile spread on his lips.

Warmth heated her cheeks, and she suddenly doubted direct challenge was the best approach with a man like Carson Nash. A man who operated in the gray area just outside the law.

She opened her mouth to protest, but it was too late to recant.

Carson raised her chin with his fingers, his touch less than forceful but more than casual. He brushed his lips against hers, sending a torrent of heat through her body.

He pulled back as if he'd touched a hot stove.

Ava sucked in a breath attempting to cool the fire in her veins, but it wouldn't be doused.

She gazed up at him, caught in the moment and lost in a hazy memory she couldn't quite grasp.

His assault on her emotions continued. In

one urgent move, he pulled her onto his lap and kissed her again.

Embarrassment oozed from every pore in her body as she pulled out of the kiss and met the stares of the passengers seated around them. Leaning back, she turned her head toward Carson's ear. "Stop this now."

"Oh, but I can't. Not until I find what I'm after."

Panic rocketed to her nerve endings as he dipped his head and ran a bead of kisses down her neck, dipping precariously close to her cleavage.

Her body vibrated under his touch. She fought the insatiable need to respond. He wasn't ever going to stop, not until he found what he was looking for.

Several passengers stood up and moved forward, choosing seats rows ahead of the indiscreet lovers.

Ava closed her eyes as he moved his hands over every inch of her body before settling one of them on her abdomen.

Her eyes flew open. She stared up at him, trying to gauge his reaction, but there were no answers visible in his half-lidded gaze.

"Satisfied?" she asked.

He slid his hand away and stared down at her.

"Never."

She swallowed the tightness in her throat. "Everything I have on belonged to Dr. Resnick's daughter. Everything but my shoes."

His eyes narrowed. "Your service flats. Standard issue. You haven't changed them?"

"No. Resnick's daughter had feet the size of a doll, so I had to keep them on."

"Take them off." He eased her back onto the seat next to him.

Ava pulled off her shoes and put them on the seat between them.

Carson picked one up in each hand and ex-amined them.

Excitement coiled inside him as he ripped the sole liner out of the heaviest shoe.

Concealed in the heel void of the hard rubber sole was a tiny GPS unit.

"Bingo," he whispered, giving Ava a look inside before setting it down on the seat between them. "You've been tagged, probably since the morning you left in the limo."

Anger flashed in her eyes. He watched her react, and knew in that instant she'd been telling the truth.

Reaching into his pocket, he withdrew the piece of cloth he'd used to wipe down the car. He tore a thin strip off the fabric before folding it several times to thicken the layers. Next he took the tracking bug out of the shoe and placed it in the center of the cloth.

"Hold this." He put it in Ava's open palm, pulled the ends together and tied the strip of cloth around it. "Now for a ride out of here."

He turned and opened the bus window. Putting his head out, he stared at oncoming traffic, spotting his mark sitting on the other side of the intersection they were approaching.

The bus braked just as the light changed, and a red pickup pulled through the intersection.

Carson gave the package a toss as the truck, loaded down with boxes and furniture, passed by. The device landed among the moving boxes.

He pulled back inside the bus. "That should keep them busy."

He settled into the seat next to her and slipped the inner sole back into her shoe before handing it over to her.

With the tracking device gone, they'd stand a better chance. No more ambushes.

But he was wary. They weren't out of the woods yet. It was just a matter of time before the agents, loyal to an unknown enemy, caught up with them again.

He just hoped he had some answers by then and a means of counterattack.

"IT'S SPRAINED. I wrapped it up again, but she needs to stay off it as much as possible."

Carson looked at his buddy, Dr. Scott Jacobs, and felt a surge of relief. "What about the rest of her?"

"If you mean her pregnancy, she's doing great. I picked up the baby's heartbeat on Doppler, good and strong, but Ava is dehydrated and undernourished. She needs to get prenatal care as soon as possible."

Carson hung his head, feeling inadequate in his duties to her, and to his child. "The heat's on right now. As soon as I can, it's done." He looked up, studying the only man he trusted to be as far removed from the CIA's agenda as the ideologies that separated the conservatives and liberals haunting Washington, D.C., just across the Potomac.

Worry worked through him. "It's good to know she and the baby are okay."

"You better get her someplace where she can rest up. Give her lots of fluids, protein, and these prenatal vitamins." Scott handed him a sample package of pills. "Instructions are on the box. The clinic is closed tomorrow, but if there's any trouble with her ankle, I'll be in for a couple of hours early in the morning catching up on paperwork."

Carson nodded, took the vitamins and shoved them into his backpack. "I'll be in touch." He turned around and entered the exam room in the small after-hours clinic.

Ava startled and looked up as Carson came through the door. Her cheeks heated. Feeling vulnerable, she pulled the exam gown tighter around her bare body.

"Is it necessary for you to be in here?"

"Yeah." He stared straight at her, his gaze unwavering.

"Turn around, then."

"So you can clobber me again? No, thanks. Besides, I'm here to have a look at your backside."

Every muscle in Ava's body tensed. She glared at him, hoping her message got through. "You're not going to touch my back."

"The hell I'm not." He took a step toward her.

"I deserve an explanation."

"I agree." He took another step toward her, his face expressionless. "Tell me what happened in the woods outside Doc Resnick's house after the thugs caught you."

Tension closed her throat as she worked to recall their exact words. "They believed I had something that belonged to them."

"And what did they do to you once they caught you?"

Curiosity tickled over her nerves as she recalled the odd detail. "They pulled up the back of my shirt."

"And I'm going to do the same."

She sidestepped him and moved to the other side of the exam table. "This is crazy. Leave me alone, or I swear I'll scream bloody murder."

"Be my guest. The clinic is closed. Doc isn't going to challenge me. Have you forgotten the six-inch knife they planned to stick you with?"

Ava felt the blood leave her face, and braced her hands on the exam table for stability. "Never saw it."

"They were ready to carve into you. They were after something, and since they'd exposed your back, I'm going to put my money there. I'll have a look, then you can get dressed and we'll get out of here."

She gazed at him, finding a measure of reason in his request. Anything was possible...but her back?

"Okay." Reaching behind her, she secured the bottom tie on the gown and moved around the table. Turning her back to him, she untied the top fastener and pulled the gown off her shoulders before clutching it to her breasts.

Ava closed her eyes, anticipating Carson's touch. If she hoped to fight its effect on her nerves, she'd have to start well in advance of actual contact.

Desire was swift. It hit with a blow that took Carson by surprise. He stared at the curvaceous contours of Ava's back and sucked in a breath.

The creamy smooth texture of her skin sent liquid heat racing through his blood. He didn't have to touch her to conjure the memory of feeling her.

He cleared his throat and stepped forward. Reaching out, he turned on the exam light next to the table. "Bend over a bit."

She obeyed.

He adjusted the angle of the fixture, flooding the surface of her skin with light.

Something caught his eye. He rubbed his hand over a tiny scar on her skin just below her bra. "Odd. Did you cut yourself here?"

He watched gooseflesh pucker across her shoulders.

"Not that I can recall."

"Do you feel anything?" He smoothed his finger over the spot.

She flinched. "It's tender."

Pressing harder on the surface, he picked up ridging just under her skin. "There's something there."

She shuddered as she straightened and turned toward him.

"I heard the baby's heartbeat."

He wasn't prepared for the hopeful gaze she leveled on him, or the way his emotions stirred. Emotions he always kept inert.

"Doc told me."

"This afternoon, while you were hot-wiring the car, I'm sure I felt movement for the first time."

Carson's windpipe constricted. He was in uncharted waters here, and he didn't know if he could find a map, but that didn't change the fact that she was talking about his child. Their child.

"It's okay. You don't have to be excited." Disappointment contorted her face for an instant before she turned away. "I just needed to tell someone. Can I get dressed now?"

He searched for his voice, but in the end he could only turn toward the door, listening to her clothes rustle as she got dressed.

He was an idiot. A big dumb jerk. He could take out a target and make it home alive, but he couldn't offer up a fraction of emotional support for the woman carrying his baby?

"Dammit, Ava." He didn't turn around, but he was determined to apologize. To give voice to the tangle of emotions working through him. "That's great news—"

Something cracked against his skull in blinding succession. Once…twice.

Black dominated his field of vision as he tried to turn into the fight, but she'd gotten the jump on him this time.

Unable to rise out of the darkness, Carson hit the floor with a thud.

"CARSON. CAN YOU HEAR ME? Carson."

He tried to open his eyes, feeling the solid mass of floor underneath him, and hearing Scott's concerned voice.

Dragging his eyes open, he blinked until the double images came together. The back of his head throbbed like an SOB.

"Where is she?" He ground out the words as he pulled himself up into a sitting position. "Where's Ava?"

"Gone. About ten minutes ago."

He rubbed the back of his head and felt moisture. Glancing up, he noticed the missing stirrup from the exam table. She'd certainly picked a harder weapon this time than a wooden broom handle. He'd have to remember never to turn his back on her again.

"Did you see which way she went?"

"No. Sorry. I heard the front door and assumed it was both of you leaving. It wasn't until I came back here to clean up that I noticed you lying on the floor."

Carson pushed to his feet, feeling his balance stabilize. "She can't have gone far, but you'd think she'd realize by now how dangerous it is out there."

Scott held up his hand. "I don't want to hear this, Carson. I'm not with the agency anymore. The less I know, the better."

"Sorry. My mistake." Carson grabbed a handful of paper towels out of the dispenser next to the sink and soaked them under the faucet. He dabbed at the back of his head with the wad of towels.

"Let me have a look at that?"

"You've done enough, Scott. You're sure you don't know which way she went?"

"I got nothing, buddy."

Carson picked up his backpack from the

chair in the corner of the room and slung it over his shoulder. Concern and determination raged in his bloodstream as he dropped the bloody towels into the trash can and exited the exam room.

"I'll keep in touch."

Scott gave him a nod.

He strode down the hallway, out into the waiting room and out the front door.

Carson moved away from the clinic and pulled up short under an elm tree next to the street. Nighttime had settled over the city of Annandale.

Ava Ross was on her home turf. She had to be feeling safe for the first time in months. He almost didn't blame her for wanting to strike out on her own.

Almost.

Pushing away from the tree trunk, he took a right and moved down the sidewalk. Where would she go? Her parents lived in the area— she'd told him as much when they'd spent the night together. He checked his watch. He was twenty minutes away from breaking silence with his team, but he worried more about Ava as the seconds ticked by.

AVA LEANED AGAINST the side of her parents' house, listening to the familiar sounds of the night. Crickets chirped and the occasional dog barked from somewhere in the quiet neighborhood. The smell of freshly cut grass and sweet locust blossoms hung in the air.

There were no lights on, not even the porch light—something that set her nerves on edge. Maybe she should have called first, just to defer the initial shock. After all, they thought she was dead. But why hadn't she called them in the past four months?

She didn't know, but in person she would appear to be some sort of unholy apparition the first time she stepped inside, and she found herself praying she didn't give either one of them a coronary.

She pushed away from the house, staying in the shadows as she worked her way around to the back door. Maybe she should let herself in and go directly to her old room…wait until morning to give them the news.

Lifting the edge of the doormat, she fingered the key and pulled it out.

A chill ran over her skin as she straightened and surveyed the backyard right up to the tree line beyond the back fence, but she was unable to shake the odd sensation even as she shoved the key into the lock and turned it.

The door opened.

Ava pulled the key out and stashed it back under the mat, still aware of the uneasy sensation crawling along her spine. She stepped into the laundry room and closed the door, careful not to make a sound.

A wave of relief washed over her. In spite of Carson's mission to take her to McLean, she was finally home. At least to the house she'd grown up in.

A sound, deep and low caught her attention. Like a grunt or a muffled yell coming from the basement. She tried to place the noise, but couldn't.

She took a step forward.

From out of the darkness someone grabbed her.

Terror sliced into her. A scream welled in her throat as arms wrapped around her, squeezing the air out of her lungs.

Ava fought, driving her elbow into the man's ribs.

Once…twice.

But it was already too late.

Chapter Eight

Agitation coiled inside Carson as he punched in the phone number of the Lazy-B Ranch, his team's home base of operation in Idaho.

The minutes since Ava's escape were ticking by, and he knew their reprieve from pursuit was only temporary. Whatever she was involved in, whether voluntary or involuntary, her life was at risk…and the life of their child. He'd been so sure he'd convinced her of the danger, he'd let his guard down.

"Clandestine Pizza," the voice on the other end of the line said.

"I'd like to order a large sausage and mushroom to go."

"Twenty minutes."

"Can you make it ten?" Carson waited for the phone relay to go through.

"Marathon. Go ahead."

"Good to hear you, Domino. I'm in need of information ASAP." Carson relaxed a bit, but scanned the area surrounding the pay phone. "I've got a loose package. Pull her file out of the database for me, will you?"

"Hold on."

Through the phone connection, he could hear the computer keys popping.

"There's a problem. It's been locked up tight. No access."

He considered his options. Someone in the CIA had put Ava's file out of reach. Why?

"Try Samuel Ross—he's retired CIA. I couldn't get an address on him from the phone book on this end." Carson clamped his teeth together, hoping he'd remembered her father's name right. "I need his address in Annandale, Virginia."

"Looks like…what the hell!"

"Problem?"

"Someone just snagged the file."

"Did you get an address?" A knot twisted in his gut and wouldn't release.

"Yeah, barely. It's 518 Baltimore Street. He worked covert Ops for thirty years. Watch yourself."

"I'll be in touch." Carson hung up the pay phone and took off at a dead run.

AVA WAS CONSCIOUS, but didn't open her eyes. Pulling in a deep breath, she let the familiar scent of cool concrete and her mother's perfume penetrate her brain.

She was in the basement of the house, but her hands were tied, her ankles, too, and she wasn't alone. There was movement near her and muffled grunts, the same noise she'd heard when she entered the laundry room upstairs.

She swallowed and opened her eyes, fearful of what she would see, but determined to face whoever had restrained her.

Her gaze locked on the occupants of a sofa directly opposite the chair she was tied to.

Horrified, she stared at her parents. Both had their hands tied in front of them. They'd been gagged and bore the marks of a beating.

Lillian Ross's head lolled back against the sofa.

Her father sat bolt upright and yelled in spite of the gag shoved in his mouth.

She looked at her dad, full of anger, then saw him motion toward the stairwell with a tilt of his head.

A chill skittered over her nerves as she glanced in the direction he indicated, watching a long shadow move along the stairwell wall.

She'd scratch the SOB's eyes out if given the chance.

Her dad must have picked up on her rage, because when she glanced back she saw him shake his head in warning.

"Good, you're awake, Miss Ross."

Ava stiffened, staring at the man who casually stood in front of her. He was short and round, but it was the Russian accent in his deep voice that gave her a clue as to his identity. There was something familiar about him—some detail just outside her mental grasp.

"It is unfortunate you were rescued in Washington State. I lost three of my best comrades without so much as a peep from you. But now that we have your family for leverage, it's time you tell me where you've hidden the microchip."

Alarm coursed through her body. That explained why they'd kept her alive. They believed she had a chip, but they didn't know where.

It all made sense. Perfect, horrific sense.

She glanced at her parents, suddenly regretting that she'd given Carson the slip. He was the only one who could save them now.

"Boris."

Ava tensed as a bulky man stepped out of the shadows under the stairwell.

Fear flared in her father's eyes, warning her this was the muscle behind the threats.

"Don't hurt them!" she pleaded, intent on making the right choice.

"You have decided to give me the chip?"

She stared up into the man's beady black eyes. If she lied, her parents were dead. If she told the truth….

By the time they were finished digging in her back with a knife, her life would be over, but her parents would survive.

"I'll tell you where it is."

CARSON STARED at Samuel Ross's house from behind its redbrick fence. The only light came from a narrow basement window hardly big enough for a cat to squeeze through, much less a man. He'd have to find another way in, short of walking up and ringing the doorbell.

If Ava was inside, she'd be waiting for him to charge in and take her by force. And with her daddy to back her up, the whole scenario left a bad feeling in his gut.

Irritated, he braced against the solid fence, considering his options. He let his head drop back. It thumped against the bricks, making a hollow sound.

Carson pulled away, raised his hand and rapped a knuckle against the mortar. The same hollow sound echoed back to him as he moved along the barrier, ending at the corner next to the driveway.

He pulled up short, rapping back along the bricks until he heard the sound change.

It wasn't uncommon for CIA operatives to build an escape route for themselves and their families in case they were compromised at home, and Samuel Ross had certainly come up with an effective one.

A hollow fence ran around the entire perimeter of his property, the entrance to which was right in front of him.

Applying pressure, he felt the brick-covered panel give way under his hand.

It popped open, emitting the smell of damp earth.

Digging in to his pack, he pulled out a flashlight and squeezed into the narrow opening, closing it behind him.

Cobwebs dragged over him and clung to his face. He brushed them away and turned on the flashlight, shining it down the above-ground tunnel.

Admiration moved in his mind as he crawled forward. The escape tunnel was ingenious. A way for Ava's father to protect his family from harm.

Bitter memories of his own father rose inside him, enraging him.

He and Ava had grown up in two different worlds. Hers safe and loving. His violent and detrimental to everything and everyone he cared about.

Bringing his emotions under control, he pushed the rest of the way through the tunnel, intent on finding Ava and shaking some sense into her before she got herself killed.

AVA CRINGED as the brute jerked the rope from around her ankles and pulled her to her feet.

Her mother had come to and now watched through tear-filled eyes as the Russian moved toward her, a sadistic grin on his mouth. "To think we had the microchip the whole time and did not know. You could have saved yourself much pain."

"I didn't know until tonight." The memory of Carson's fingertips on her skin as he felt the scar on her back gave her pause, and hope. If ever she needed his Black Ops, bad-ass help, it was now.

The Russian studied her for a moment, a glimmer of contempt in his dark eyes. "I hope it is worth it, this death you are going to endure. Boris."

Resistance built in her body.

He untied her hands from behind her back. She was the queen of hopeless causes and she intended to earn her crown tonight.

Ava lunged for the lamp on the end table next to the sofa and grabbed it. Swinging it like a sword, she bolted for the fireplace, snagged the iron poker and dropped the lamp.

It smashed into pieces on the hardwood floor.

"Run!" she shouted to her parents, hopefully buying enough time for them to escape, but only her mother hobbled toward the stairs. Her father stayed for the fight.

She watched in horror as the bulky man head-butted him.

Her dad reeled back onto the sofa, gasping for air.

There were worse ways to die; at least she'd go out fighting.

Like scavengers on a kill, the two men stalked her, backing her up against the fireplace. "I lied. The microchip is hidden at my house. If you don't back off, you'll never retrieve it."

"Now you are lying. I have been to your house. I have searched your house. There is no chip there."

Ava swallowed. The jig was up, but not until she wreaked some havoc of her own.

She moved right, swung the poker and caught the bulky Russian on the forearm as he raised it to protect himself.

Pulling the poker away, she jerked it back to the left, but the ringleader ducked. The blow sliced the air above his head.

His cohort rushed her, locked her in a bear hug and squeezed the air out of her lungs.

An instant of blackness blanketed her before she hit the ground. The sound of ripping fabric and cool air on her skin rocked her senses.

She attempted to move, but the men held her down on the floor.

"Let her go!"

The sound of Carson's voice laced with malice came from somewhere in the room.

Ava closed her eyes.

She heard the snap of a switchblade, but it was the feel of cold steel on her skin that froze her in place.

Pop! Pop! Carson double tapped the big man with the blade against Ava's back, but not before a crimson trail of blood welled on her skin.

Half a second later he double tapped the smaller man next to him.

Fighting a tangle of irrational emotions, he charged forward, intent on her still body lying facedown.

Was he too late? His heart jolted as he crashed to his knees next to her. She'd been nicked with the knife, but it was a minor wound.

In slow motion he watched her move, and helped her turn over in his arms. She stared up at him, her look of horror subsiding along with his heart rate.

"Ava…" His throat closed and he pulled her into his arms before anger oozed up from inside him and intensified his reaction.

"You could have been killed." He stared into her upturned face. "If you ever do that again—"

"I know what they want. There's a microchip implanted under my skin."

Carson closed his eyes for an instant and put his anger aside. Holding her was the only thing he wanted to do, but he sobered and shoved his 9 mm into its holster with his free hand.

The sound of her father's voice cut into Ava's brain, even while the feel of Carson's protective arms relaxed her. She watched as Carson went to her parents to remove their gags and untie their hands.

A sob started deep in her chest and rattled her body as she came to her feet with Carson's help and embraced her parents.

"I'm sorry," she whispered, letting her emotions go, "that you had to find out like this."

"We've known for a couple of hours that you were still alive."

"We're just glad you're here, honey," her mom said, brushing the hair out of her eyes as if she was a child again.

"Is that how long they've been here?" She motioned to the two dead men, sprawled in front of the fireplace.

"Yeah. They ambushed us in our bed. There was nothing I could do. They said they wanted you."

"That's when they told us you weren't on the plane when it went down." Her mom locked her hand on Ava's arm before giving her another hug.

"We have you to thank." Samuel Ross turned to Carson and extended his hand. "I don't know what the hell you're doing in my basement, but I'm glad you're here."

Carson shook Samuel Ross's hand, feeling the man's iron grip. "Agent Carson Nash."

Samuel Ross's eyes narrowed for a moment. "Nice operation, Agent, but you need to take my daughter and get out of here. My wife put out an emergency call. An insurrection team will be here in a matter of minutes."

Carson stiffened. The worst thing that could happen was for them to be tagged by an insurrection team.

Ava's nerves pulled tight as she looked back and forth at the two most important men in her life. Her gaze settled on her father.

"I'm not leaving you."

"Do your old man a favor and get moving. You're safer on the outside with Agent Nash."

Ava felt the blood leave her face and puddle in her toes.

"Do you trust him?" her father asked.

She considered her dad's question, searching for the answer in her heart. "Yes."

"Then let him help you." Samuel Ross shoved his hands into his pockets.

Carson took Ava's hand in his and steered her toward the stairwell, taking the steps two at a time.

He pulled her along the hall and out into the living room, stopping at the door of the coat closet.

"How did you find this?" she asked. "It's a secret."

"I guessed and it paid off. Your dad planned ahead."

Ava had never really known what her father had done for the CIA for thirty years, and she was suddenly glad she'd been left blissfully in the dark. But she was glad he'd provided an escape route for his family.

Carson pulled open the closet door and they stepped inside.

Feeling around the back of the closet, she found the latch and turned it. The spring-loaded exit panel popped open.

A shiver rattled her, but she followed him through the opening, putting aside all thought of what might have taken up residence in the narrow aboveground passage.

Carson switched on the flashlight and aimed it at the exit panel less than fifty feet in front of them.

The Russians liked to work in three-man teams. With two dead in the Rosses' basement, that left one to keep watch somewhere on the outside.

"How'd you get into the house?" he asked over his shoulder.

"Back door. There's a key under the mat."

"Did you see anyone?"

"No. I mean…I could swear I was being watched. It was just a feeling, but…"

"They travel in three-man teams. They've probably got a lookout posted on the perimeter."

Carson paused next to the exit panel, drew his weapon and killed the light. "The street's too exposed. He's got to be on the perimeter. Stay here. I'll come back for you as soon as I secure the area."

A chill ran down her back and she fought

the urge to look behind into the darkness. "Okay."

"Hang tight." Carson pushed the panel, letting in a breath of fresh air, but the panel closed just as quickly and she regretted that she hadn't asked for the flashlight.

Ava hunkered down, refusing to let the tight quarters and her rising panic get the upper hand. Carson had said he would return for her and she knew he would.

But what if he didn't? What if there were threats out there he didn't know about?

Worry sliced through her. What would it hurt if she waited outside in the dark? The lookout was somewhere in the backyard, according to Carson.

If she stayed next to the exit panel she'd be well out of the Russian's territory.

A wave of dizziness washed over her, making her stomach pinch. She was going to be sick. She had to get out of the claustrophobic tunnel before she went berserk.

Desperate for escape, she reached out and pushed the panel with her hands.

It gave against the pressure and popped open an inch.

She put her eye to the crack and stared out into the night, ignoring the thud of her heartbeat. Taking a deep breath of fresh air, she worked to keep her nerves under control.

The quiet residential street appeared deserted in her limited field of vision; she needed desperately to breathe.

Pressing forward, she squeezed out of the opening and closed the panel. Being crouched next to the wall made her feel a lot less like a sardine in a can.

Her head cleared.

She relaxed, looking up and down the street. Nothing. No sign of movement.

The thump of footfalls to her right in the driveway sent sudden terror streaking through her.

Was it Carson?

She didn't know, but she sure wasn't going to wedge herself back in the tunnel. Her best option was to follow the fence to the corner, then bolt across the street and take cover among a row of parked cars. Beyond that lay a park. She could hunker down there until the danger passed.

Armed with a plan, she crept along the

brick fence, listening as the footsteps stopped.

A row of mature trees inside the yard offered additional protection as she reached the end of the fence.

Ava hesitated, listening for the sound of pursuit.

Slowly she straightened under the protective canopy of branches and leaves to get a better view.

There was 150 feet of open territory between her and the cars. Plenty of time for the Russian's lookout to get a bead on her.

Anticipation pricked her nerves as she focused on the location she planned to target.

In one fell swoop a strong arm locked around her body. A hand clamped over her mouth and she was lifted into the tree above.

Scrabbling for footing, she found a tree limb as her captor pulled her against his chest and went still higher in the dense leaves of the maple.

Ava closed her eyes as her captor's familiar scent invaded her senses.

He'd found her out.

Carson pulled in a breath and surveyed the area through the leaves of the tree. He watched a man climb over the fence at the northwest corner of the yard, an assault rifle in his hands.

"Don't move or make a sound," he whispered in Ava's ear, satisfied when she nodded. "There's a sniper heading our way." He felt her shudder against him and tightened his hold on her.

The adversary wore night-vision goggles, but they were safe in the tree, high above his line of sight.

Beads of sweat welled on Carson's forehead as he removed his hand from Ava's mouth and followed the sniper's movements across the yard before losing him in the shadows at the end of the house less than fifty feet away. He waited for the sniper to reappear and discover his dead comrade lying under the maple tree.

Carson took aim with his weapon, his muscles knotted with tension.

The sniper materialized at the corner of the house.

Carson watched the sniper's head movements as he looked back and forth, scanning the yard for signs of movement through the night-vision goggles.

The sniper moved into range, spotting his comrade. He rushed forward.

Carson squeezed the trigger twice in rapid succession.

The sniper dropped.

Chapter Nine

Carson let out the breath he'd been holding, but didn't release his grip on Ava. "I told you to stay put. He could have killed you," he whispered against her ear, sucking in the scent of night air on her skin. Longing invaded his body.

"I couldn't stay in that dank tunnel another minute. I was going to be sick."

"That dank tunnel was the only protection you had." Anger pushed his words out, making them sound harsh in his own ears.

"I know," she whispered.

His anger evaporated, but the desire stayed.

"We got one sure thing tonight," he said, trying not to enjoy the feel of her next to him in the tree.

"What's that?"

"We know what's under your skin." Carson sobered. There wasn't a chance their pursuers would stop until they recovered the chip from her.

It would help if they knew who'd planted it, but the information was still locked in her head.

Carson scanned the area.

Satisfied it was safe, he worked his way down out of the tree and waited for Ava, who stepped from branch to branch. He reached up and helped her down.

Taking her hand, he took one last look around and moved out of the shadows, making for the sidewalk on the other side of the street. Slowing his pace, he took up a nonchalant gait next to her.

"Just a couple of lovers out for a late-night stroll?" she asked beside him.

"Something like that. Running could draw attention. That's the last thing we need right now." He made for the car he'd acquired and opened the passenger door for her. She climbed in. He went around to the driver's side, eyeing the street with caution.

He climbed in and shoved the key into the ignition. The engine fired up.

"A key? I'm impressed. Where'd you get this one?"

He threw her a sideways glance. "A company motor pool garage. I took it from the key box. No one is going to miss it until the day after tomorrow."

"Tomorrow?" There was confusion in her voice. Hell, he'd lost track of time himself.

"Fourth of July holiday."

"Oh."

The silence was deafening as Carson put the car in Drive and pulled away from the curb. He waited until he'd turned the corner before he flipped on the headlights.

"It's okay. After what you've been through the calendar hardly seems relevant."

"My parents used to take me to the national mall every Fourth for the fireworks."

He homed in on the melancholy in her voice. "Our firecracker fix was the city park."

"Where'd you grow up?" she asked.

"A little town outside Dallas called Wylie,

near Lake Lavon." Those were the good times, Carson decided as he let the memories slip through his mind. As opposed to the bad times, which were too numerous to count.

He turned down the street one block over.

"Where are we going?"

"Dr. Resnick said you might have some recall if you were exposed to familiar places. I thought we'd take a swing past your house."

"My house?"

He braked at a stop sign and looked over at her.

"You don't live far from here."

She turned wide eyes on him. "I can't even remember the address."

"I've got it right here." Digging in to his pants pocket, he pulled out the mangled business card she'd given him four months ago, glad he hadn't followed his gut and tossed it into the trash.

He handed it to her, and this time she took it.

Ava straightened the card and stared at it. The telephone number was familiar, but the address wasn't. "You're sure Resnick would want me to go here?"

"It's worth a try. Right now we've got nothing on the bogeys that keep tracking us down."

She didn't get anything, not so much as a hint of recognition from the address— 811 Ohio. Maybe actually seeing the house would produce results.

"Your parents took the information you were still alive pretty well."

"Considering they had to hear it from a Russian agent who was assaulting them. Yeah."

"You never contacted them after you escaped in Seattle?"

"I guess not. Weird, huh?"

"Doc Resnick said the blocks would prevent you from recalling simple information, like phone numbers."

"My dad and I are close. He'd be the first person I'd contact in a crisis."

"You must have spent most of the time running, or someone would have recovered the chip from you."

Ava's heart rate kicked up. "The memories

are spotty. I don't know how I managed to survive."

"Is there any way your father could be involved?"

Anger gripped her body and she turned on him. "No way! He'd never hurt me."

"Sorry. I had to ask. Whatever is going on, there's someone on the inside calling the shots."

She tried to make sense out of what he was saying, and let her ire deflate. If only she could remember who'd been in the limo that morning.

"Any idea how we're going to remove the chip?"

"Yeah." Carson took a left onto Ohio.

"I'm going to get in touch with Doc Jacobs tomorrow morning. You're going to need a local and a skilled hand to get it out."

"What then?"

"We find someone to run an analysis on it. If we can determine what's on it, we'll have a better chance of discovering who implanted it."

Ava nodded.

Carson glanced over at her in the confines

of the moving car. She was tense. He could see it in the set of her shoulders, and he wished he could help ease her worries somehow. The stress couldn't be good for her, or the baby.

He slowed the car and pulled in next to the curb across the street from her small cottage-style home, with a For Sale sign in the front yard.

The neighborhood was quiet. He scanned the street, convinced they hadn't been followed. Still, he'd use extreme caution just in case.

"There it is." He pointed.

Ava stared at the quaint house, searching her mind for any sort of recognition. "It's perfect. I'd live there."

"You do live there. I looked out that window the morning you left. Do you remember?"

"A curtain. I remember seeing a curtain move." Sharp pain throbbed in her head. Fighting a wave of nausea, she closed her eyes. "Can we go inside?"

"Do you have a key?"

"I'm fresh out."

Excitement puckered her nerves as she climbed out of the car and met Carson in the street.

"Take it easy. We don't want your neighbors to think the place is being broken into. The cops will be all over it."

She contained her energy, taking his hand as they walked across the dark street. Pausing, she stared at the For Sale sign in the front yard, feeling a measure of sadness.

"I should have asked my parents about the house. What if I don't live here anymore?"

"Relax." Carson's nerves felt frayed. "I'd bet they just put it on the market. It's got to be empty."

Ava was silent as they walked up the driveway and around to the French doors in back.

Carson put his pack down on a patio chair and dug out the flashlight.

"Same chairs, just as I remember." Taking a step forward, he turned on the light and shone it into the vacant house.

The flashlight beam illuminated the interior, casting strange shadows on the furniture.

Ava stood, her face inches from the glass as she stared inside. Brief flashes of memory zipped through her head. Doing dishes at the kitchen sink, flipping on the TV, running up the stairs—but nothing about the damn limo.

"Anything?" Carson asked.

"I have great taste."

He turned off the light, and her hope went out along with it.

"Can we go? I don't feel so good."

"Headache?"

"Yeah."

"Resnick said you'd experience them."

Carson took her hand again, giving it a squeeze. She'd had enough trauma for one night.

Ping!

A bullet shattered a pane in the French doors.

Ava screamed.

He pulled her down onto the patio deck and unholstered his 9 mm.

Staring into the darkness, he tried to pinpoint where the shot had come from. His guess was a bank of trees directly behind the house.

"Let's get out of here."

Grabbing her hand, they bolted for the corner of the house.

A shot drilled into the siding just above their heads.

"Run!" Carson yelled as he thrust Ava into the driveway and squeezed off two shots, aimed at the bank of trees.

A flash of return fire shone against the darkness, nailing the shooter's location.

Carson steadied himself against the corner of the house and took aim.

Pop! Pop! He fired two rounds.

A groan sounded in the night somewhere near the edge of the lawn.

Carson pulled back, almost catching Ava as she raced for the car parked in the street.

They jumped in.

He fired the engine and stomped on the gas pedal. The tires spun, grabbing asphalt as they shot away from the curb.

He didn't slow until they reached the end of the street.

Feathering the brake, he whipped around the corner, making sure they weren't being followed.

"They're everywhere. Where are we going to hide?"

Carson considered their options, finally landing on the only one he had left.

"We're going to McLean."

The air in the car became charged. "You said—"

"I have a safe house there. I always figured I'd be better off sitting on the CIA's doorstep in a crisis."

"I hope you're right."

"How about a late-night dinner? I promised Scott I'd take care of you." Changing the subject seemed to relax her.

"Red meat, please," she said.

He looked over at her and smiled. He didn't understand pregnancy—in fact, he didn't know a damn thing about it—but he was willing to learn.

Carson scanned the main drag and spotted an open fast-food joint. He pulled into the parking lot and rolled around to the drive-up window, where he ordered burgers, fries and drinks. "You need to get some rest."

"Your total is $13.68, sir. Please pull forward to the first window."

She looked at him for a moment and he witnessed a flash of fear in her eyes. "That'd be good. My ankle is swollen. I need to get off it."

Did she trust him to take care of her? Apparently not, judging by the night's events.

Carson let up on the brake and pulled up to the window. Digging out his wallet, he paid for the food and accepted the take-out bags from a teenager.

He passed the food over to Ava and pulled out of the drive-up window and out into the street.

"We've got to come to an agreement." He resisted the urge to rub the back of his head where she'd clobbered him less than two hours ago.

"I want to make it out of this thing alive and I know you do, too." He glanced over at her, trying to gauge her acceptance of the situation. "My neck's on the chopping block, now that I've chosen to hang on to you. My director is going to be all over this by morning. Once he demands I complete the mission and bring you in, and I don't comply, I'll be declared rogue."

"You'd do that for me?"

"I already have, but you have to trust me, Ava. No more surprise attacks. I can't protect you if you won't let me." He narrowed his eyes, watching her face register emotion. Worry, guilt and finally resolve.

"I'm sorry for taking you out at the doctor's office. I don't know why, but I needed to get to my parents."

"I understand."

"No more escape plans. I promise. Cross my heart." She made an *X* gesture on her chest and he accepted her promise for the time being.

By tomorrow there'd be a pack of CIA agents raining down on them like a hailstorm, and he was determined to make sure Ava and his child weren't in the deluge.

CARSON TURNED ON the light and stepped into the tiny apartment. He searched all rooms before giving Ava the okay to enter.

The place cost him a small fortune every

month, but it was off grid and untraceable, a fact that could keep them both alive.

Ava came in out of the hallway with the food bags in her hands. Her face was drawn with exhaustion, her steps sluggish.

A twist of worry knotted his stomach.

She was tough, but the need to protect her from further harm morphed into an overwhelming desire to hold her.

Carson shoved the feeling aside, closed the apartment door and secured the dead bolt before turning back into the room and dropping his pack on the couch.

"Let's eat."

She'd already taken the food out of the bags and was arranging it on the tiny dining table in the corner next to the galley kitchen.

He pulled out a chair and sat down, feeling the stress in his body dissipate.

He opened his burger and bit into it, watching her devour her food like a hungry lioness. He needed to take better care of her. Three square meals a day, plenty of water and the vitamins Doc Jacobs had given her.

"Scott gave you some prenatal vitamins." He stood up, grabbed his backpack off the sofa and opened the bag. Reaching in, he pulled out the box of pills and brought them to the table. "Probably better with food."

Ava took them in one hand, then laid them on the table. "Thanks," she said between bites.

He had to smile as he watched her pop the last of her burger into her mouth and chew. "You weren't kidding about that red meat thing, were you?"

She grinned at him and he felt his heart rate pick up.

"That was spectacular." She leaned back in her chair and wiped her mouth with a napkin. "I can't keep running. How long before my body decides enough is enough and takes it out on my baby?" Ava blinked, her eyes glazed with tears.

"I'll be here." He fixed a stare on her. "I've got a stake in what happens to you, and our…child."

He moved toward her, intent on alleviating her concerns, even though the same worries pounded in his head.

"Take it easy." He wrapped his arms around her slender body, feeling her tense, then relax. "It'll be over soon." His own words echoed in his ears as he pulled back and stared into her eyes. "Get some sleep. We'll regroup in the morning."

She nodded, then reached up to smooth her hand down his cheek.

Desire, hot and unreasonable, turned his blood to fire in his veins. He stared at her lips, unable to deny the attraction that sizzled between them like lightning to ground.

"Dammit, Ava," he whispered as he leaned in and brushed her lips with his.

Like a dam breaking, liquid fire washed through him in a torrent. He deepened the kiss, listening to the uneven sound of her breathing.

He ended the kiss and rocked back, staring at her for a moment before running his hand over his head as he tried to corral his outlaw thoughts.

He stood up, reluctantly putting distance between them.

Ava braced herself, mesmerized by the depth of desire she'd felt move through her body. If there had been any doubt they'd been together before, it vanished in that instant.

She stared at him from across the room. If only her memory would substantiate what her body already seemed to know.

"Where do I sleep?" She tried to slow her pounding heart rate, to sound casual, but her voice quivered.

"You take the bedroom. I'll sleep on the couch."

She turned away from him, afraid to give voice to the feelings and sensations stirring in her blood. It was safer to retreat. Safer to squash the emotions that would only lead to trouble with a man like Carson Nash. A man with a secret life and no room for a woman and child.

"Good night," she whispered as she went into the bedroom and closed the door behind her.

CARSON TRIED TO FOCUS as he dialed the number for the Lazy-B, his lifeline to information.

The feel of Ava in his arms was still fresh, even though she'd gone to bed over an hour ago.

"Clandestine Pizza."

"I'd like a large sausage and mushroom to go."

"That'll be twenty minutes."

"Can you make it ten?" Carson waited for the call to be routed and relaxed when he heard Agent Nick Shelby on the other end of the line.

"Marathon. Where the hell are you? The director has been in overdrive trying to locate you and the package."

"There's been a development with the mission."

"Do you want me to pass that along?"

"Negative. I'll take care of it myself. I need info tonight." He felt wary as he considered the trouble he might bring down on his team, but he had to know what was going on.

"Go ahead, Marathon."

"What can you find on the name Hinshaw? Limit your search to the eastern seaboard, D.C. and the surrounding areas. Archives, too, at least six months back."

"Copy that." The click of computer keys rattled over the phone line.

Carson pulled in a breath, hoping the name meant something and they'd get a hit.

"There was a story March tenth in the *Boston Globe*. MIT student Jerome Hinshaw disappeared outside of his Pacific Street dorm. No one has seen or heard from him since March first. The local police are investigating."

"Does it say what his field of expertise is?"

"He was a top-notch student working on research involving satellite technology. That's it."

Carson considered the implications of the information. "Fax me a picture of him ASAP."

"I'll see what I can find. What's the number?"

Carson rattled off the number to his secure landline.

"FYI. I'll probably be declared rogue in the a.m. Don't buy a word of it."

There was silence on the other end of the line for a second. "Hate to tell you, but it's a done deal."

Carson sucked in a breath and let it out. The wheels of the spy world turned quickly. "Who gave the order?"

"The director. You're to be taken alive along with your package."

Regret burned into him. He'd been declared by his own director, he only hoped he could patch up his reputation when this whole thing was over.

"Thanks for the heads-up. I'll be in touch." He hung up the telephone. He needed to be prepared for the worst.

Rogue could spell death. He'd become a marked man, a target for any CIA personnel who wanted to take a crack at him. But it was Ava he worried about the most, and the child inside her.

His child.

Chapter Ten

Carson maneuvered the car through light traffic and braked at a stoplight. The fourth of July holiday had come on a weekday and things were at a standstill.

"You look good this morning." He glanced over at Ava, noting the pink in her cheeks and a sparkle in her eyes.

"I slept like a baby. Something I haven't done for a while."

The light changed.

He accelerated. "How did you survive in Seattle for four months?"

"I know I spent some time in motels for a couple of weeks after I got off the airplane. I had receipts in my pockets. Then my cash ran out. I suppose it took the Agency a couple of weeks to discover I wasn't killed in the crash and less time for the Russians, considering the plane went down in the Bering Strait in their airspace. Not long after that they started to hunt me. I survived in the streets until the Russians found me."

"I'm betting the GPS wasn't activated until after you arrived in Seattle and the plane went down. When your body wasn't recovered from the wreckage, that's when the GPS was activated and you were discovered. What made you get off the plane in the first place?"

"I knew something had happened. I remembered getting into the limo. The next thing I remembered I was leaving my seat for the lavatory on board the jet. I also knew I'd recently been with someone." She stared over at him. "A woman knows these things."

Carson's heart slammed into his ribs as he recalled the night in question with too much clarity. "You looked up at me just before you got into the car. Do you remember?"

"Looking up, yes. At you. No." Her cheeks flamed hot and pink.

He reached over and touched her hand. "It

was consensual, Ava. I'd never force a woman to do anything she didn't want to do."

A chill quaked inside her as she considered the information. Making love with Carson that night had saved her life. If it had never happened, she would have stayed on the plane that crashed. She'd be dead now.

She swallowed the lump in her throat. "I thought I'd been slipped a roofie because I couldn't remember that night. I planned to go to the authorities in Seattle." She looked over at him. "I'm glad I was wrong."

"Me, too," he said.

She fought the urge to touch him and turned back, staring at the road ahead. "None of that explains the microchip I've got under my skin."

"We'll get answers once we get to the doctor's office and he removes it. I'll have it analyzed, find out what's on it. The information could lead us in the right direction."

"I hope so. Carrying a foreign body around with me isn't my idea of fun, especially when agents with knives want to remove it so badly they're willing to do anything."

"I contacted a member of my team last night. The name Hinshaw belongs to an MIT student, Jerome Hinshaw. He disappeared around the same time you got on the plane."

She worked the timeline in her head. "He could have been in the car that morning. Maybe that's where I heard the name." Her heart rate sped up, her throat tightened. "Have they found him?"

"Still missing."

Was that the stressor that had put her over the edge? Had she witnessed Jerome Hinshaw's demise in the back of the limo?

Fear stirred her thoughts and she prayed it wasn't true. Even though she knew it would explain some things, it didn't explain her loss of memory or the reason behind it.

Ava stared out the car window, trying to alleviate her fear. Carson was next to her. He'd protect her—she knew that now.

Carson turned into the clinic parking lot and pulled around back. Doc's red BMW was sitting in its parking space behind the building.

"He's here. Let's get this done." He climbed

out of the car and walked around to Ava's side. He opened the car door and helped her out.

Her once-pink cheeks blanched.

"You're not afraid of a little incision, are you?"

"No."

"So why do you look like you've seen a ghost?"

"It's called morning sickness."

A hedge of embarrassment skimmed his nerves. "Are you going to be all right?"

"Yeah. I just need a minute." She leaned against the car, sucking in several deep breaths. "Better."

Carson put his arm around her waist and moved forward, glad her coloring had returned by the time they reached the rear entrance to the clinic.

He paused at the back door and peeked through the glass. Reaching down, he tried the knob. The door was locked.

He knocked several times. Scott's office was just down the hall—certainly he could hear if someone was at the door.

Looking down, Carson spotted a doorbell and pressed it.

The sound of the chimes echoed inside the clinic, but Scott didn't answer.

"Something's wrong." He stared through the glass. Then he took Ava's hand and led her along the back of the building, stopping at the window in the middle.

The shades were open.

At the edge of the window frame he leaned in for a look.

Scott Jacobs was slumped over his desk. His office had been trashed.

"He's inside. He's not moving. We've got to get in there."

They hurried back to the door.

Carson pulled his shirtsleeve down over his hand and broke a panel in the door glass with a punch.

Reaching inside, he turned the lock on the doorknob and pushed the door open before pulling his 9 mm from his ankle holster.

"Stay behind me. There could still be someone inside the building."

Ava stood close behind him. Reaching back, he touched her as he moved into the door frame and shot a glance in both directions.

It was clear.

Moving out into the hallway, he took a left and worked his way to the waiting room. Scanning the empty space, he nodded to her and turned back toward the hallway lined with exam rooms and Scott's office. He cleared the first room on the left.

Exam rooms two and three were also clear. Lastly he cleared Scott's office. "Wait out here."

Ava nodded.

Carson didn't have to take Scott's pulse to know he was dead, but he did it anyway. Reaching around from behind, he felt for a carotid pulse. Nothing.

There was no apparent sign of trauma... until he took a closer look at Scott's neck.

Cold understanding sobered him as he examined the telltale bruising. It was an Agency-style kill. Dr. Scott Jacobs's neck had been snapped, and he was still warm.

Cautiously Carson moved toward the hallway where he'd left Ava.

He stepped into the hall, but it was empty.

In the direction of the back door he heard the crush of shoes on broken glass.

The hair at his nape bristled.

He raised his gun and moved toward the sound. Maybe she'd decided to step out. Was she feeling sick again?

He stopped next to the door frame, listening for movement, then stepped into the doorway, only to find the entrance empty and the back door standing open.

Carson bolted through the door just in time to see a flash near the edge of the parking lot. Rushing forward, he dived into the bushes for cover, catching sight of Ava being manhandled by a man dressed in black.

Rage exploded inside him. He lunged forward, catching the thug in the back.

The man fell forward, losing his grip on Ava.

She stumbled, fell to the ground and crawled away from the fight.

"You SOB," Carson yelled as he worked to restrain the thug from behind before he turned on him.

Only the flash of a knife blade gave him

pause, and only for a moment. He slammed his booted foot into the man's chest.

The knife hit the dirt.

One more kick and the man slumped to the ground, his eyes narrowed and piercing as he stared up at Carson, then at the gun in his hand.

"Who are you?" Carson demanded.

For an instant fear flashed in the man's dark eyes. He was most likely CIA, a part of the squad ordered to bring them in. But how had he gotten the information about Scott?

There were only a couple of people who knew Scott was ex-CIA and a friendly.

Caution and mistrust worked his muscles into knots as he stared down at the agent, deciding what to do with him. His friend was dead, and all because he'd chosen to help them.

Angrily Carson pulled the man to his feet and searched him for weapons, finding a pistol in his shoulder holster and another one strapped to his ankle.

Someone had to pay for killing Scott Jacobs, and he planned to find out who the SOB was.

CARSON GRIPPED the steering wheel so hard his hands throbbed. He'd have given anything to have spared Ava the trauma of witnessing, or at least hearing, his interrogation of the agent who'd killed Scott Jacobs, but it couldn't be helped.

In the end the man had given him nothing. He was no closer to finding out what was going on than he'd been days ago.

"He'll make it, Ava. Once the cops get there and call EMS, he'll do fine." He glanced over at her placid features, profiled against the car window, and took a deep breath. He wasn't always happy with the terms of his job, especially when he couldn't produce results.

"I know," she whispered. "He did kill your friend and try to take me. If you hadn't stopped him, I'd probably be dead, too."

Carson drove into the parking garage of the apartment complex, pulled into a space and killed the engine.

"He was there looking for the chip, assuming Scott had already removed it. When he didn't find it or the answers he wanted, he killed him. We walked into it."

"You have to take this thing out of me." She looked over at him, her expression hopeful, the corners of her mouth turned up in a tight smile. "That's the only way we're going to know what's on it and what value it has."

Worry ground through him. "Can't do it. It's too close to your spine. The only person who's going to retrieve it is a doctor."

"I understand." She pulled the door handle and climbed out of the car.

Carson met her and they walked to the elevator for the ride up to the third floor. "I've got a fax of Jerome Hinshaw coming in. Have a look, see if it jogs anything in your memory."

She stepped into the elevator with him. "Of course. But I don't know what good it'll do."

"We've got nothing, Ava, and the odds are good that things are going to get a lot hotter. I've been declared a rogue."

Her head jerked up, and a moment of terror blazed in her eyes. "They really do that?"

"When an agent skips out on a mission

with his package in tow. Yeah. The good news is that I'm to be taken alive."

He heard her sharp intake of breath.

"That beats the alternative."

Carson was alert for any sign of trouble as the elevator doors slid open and they exited, making their way to the end of the hall. He pulled the key from his pocket, unlocked the apartment door and followed Ava inside.

"We're going to be fine." He met her where she stood next to the sofa and grasped her shoulders in his hands. "As long as we keep a low profile, they're not going to find us. This apartment is secure—I made sure of it."

Worry drew her eyebrows together. "It's hard to dig for answers while you're lying low."

He considered her summation. It was true. If they couldn't maneuver, they couldn't discover the truth.

The sound of the phone, followed by the fax machine engaging, pulled him out of his thoughts. "Our snapshot of Jerome Hinshaw." He walked over to the desk.

Ava moved up next to Carson, watching the fax roll out of the machine.

A rush of excitement filled her, but it was quickly followed by a wave of horror as the face materialized before her eyes, bringing a flood of memories with it.

She stepped back. Nausea whirled in her stomach and threatened to overwhelm her, but she fought it.

"It's him. I saw him in the limo when I climbed in."

Carson was next to her in an instant. He helped her into a chair at the table.

"What do you remember?" He squatted next to her, watching her with intense blue eyes.

"Stabbed. He was stabbed in the back of the car. We were moving. I can hear him pleading for his life, but they wouldn't stop."

She looked at him, wishing the horrific images were gone again. "There were two other men in the car with us. I can see the knife plunging into Hinshaw. One, two… three times. There's blood everywhere. That's all I remember. Then everything goes dark until I wake up on the airplane."

Fear twisted inside her as she leaned toward Carson, feeling his arms come around her.

She buried her face against his shoulder, letting his strength and proximity soothe her, even while his scent invaded her senses, awakening need deep inside her body.

He stroked her back, sending ripples of pleasure through her as she pushed back from him and gazed into his face.

There was determination in the hard set of his jaw. She refocused on his lips, wanting to feel them against her own with a desire that laced through her entire body taking every nerve ending captive.

Heat flamed in her cheeks as she leaned closer, satisfied when he did the same. Was he caught in the torrent with her? Drawn to the fire she could feel igniting every hollow in her body?

Ava anticipated the kiss as they came together. Her breath caught in her throat. He parted her lips, pushing his tongue into her mouth. She opened for him, tasting him as the kiss deepened. Her mind went blank, all thought erased by a passion that consumed her. She clung to him, hungry for more. Hungry to feel him against her bare skin. Hungry for the memories of the night they'd spent together four months ago.

He shuddered and ended the kiss, pulling back from her before cupping her face in both his hands. His eyes narrowed as he looked at her. A muscle worked along his jawline. His breathing was uneven, so close she could feel it against her skin.

She closed her eyes, fighting the overwhelming desire aroused by his touch.

They were on a mission, but she couldn't help wishing things were different. That their lives weren't in danger. That her memory was intact.

Carson stared at Ava's beautiful face and watched her eyelids flutter open.

His heart hammered against his ribs as he tried to deny the insatiable craving anchored deep in his soul.

She was vulnerable right now. The memory of seeing Hinshaw die had upset her and driven her into his arms. He'd be a jerk to take advantage of her in her current state.

He let his hands drop from her face and stood up, taking the chair across from her at the dining-room table. Disappointment flooded his body as the moment passed.

"How would you feel about a road trip?"

She stared at him as if he'd lost his mind or grown two heads. "Jerome Hinshaw?"

"Yeah. If we can get into his dorm room, or talk to some of his research buddies, maybe we can discover exactly what he was working on when he disappeared."

"Leverage?"

He liked the way her mind worked. "That's about all we can hope for, sweetheart. Maybe we can use it to secure your safety."

"What about you?"

"Don't worry about me." He grinned, glad when she smiled back at him, but they were about to play a very dangerous game. The stakes? Possibly their lives.

"I've got to make a phone call." He pulled his cell off his belt and wandered into the kitchen before punching in Dr. Resnick's number.

Ava's breakthrough couldn't be ignored.

A mechanical answering-machine voice came over the handset. He waited for the message to end. The beep came shortly after.

"Doc. Ava had a breakthrough. She remembered a murder in the backseat of a limo, a man named Jerome Hinshaw. We're headed for Cambridge, Massachusetts, to see what we can find out about him.

"Give me a call. I need to know if there's anything else I can do to help her recall who else was in the car that morning."

Chapter Eleven

"Take a right on Western Avenue." Ava rechecked the map in her hand before looking up, searching for the road sign. "There."

"Got it." Carson turned onto the tree-lined street that would take them to the MIT campus. It was a long shot, but it was the only one they had that didn't include a team of pistol-packing agents, determined to kill them and carve into Ava on sight.

"We're looking for the Pacific Street dormitory." He watched her stare at the map and look up again as they passed several streets.

"Take Massachusetts Avenue."

Signaling, he turned left, slowing for a student on a bike.

"It's summer, you know." She gave him a sideways glance.

"I know, but the summer session is in and there's a chance we can get into his dorm room. Maybe talk to his roommate. Or better yet, have a look at his computer files."

"That's too many maybes for me. Have we driven 450 miles for nothing?" She gave him an exasperated look and shook her head.

"I phoned ahead, sweetheart."

She smiled and turned away.

An odd sensation settled in his chest. The trip had taken some of the fear out of her. Putting four hundred-plus miles between them and the CIA was just what Ava needed.

Ava continued giving him directions, and in a few minutes they were pulling to a stop in the dorm parking lot.

"Have you got your ID?"

"Yeah." She pulled it out of her pocket and flipped it open, staring at the name again. "FBI agent Mary Walker." She plastered a serious look on her face and turned to him, repeating the name and title several times.

Carson stifled a chuckle as he listened to

her voice rise and fall with the official declaration.

"Convincing?" she asked.

He stared at her perfect lips for a second too long before answering. "It'll do, but I don't anticipate much resistance. We'll either get the information or we won't."

"Okay, Agent…?"

"Daniels," he said as he climbed out of the car and shut the door. "Mike Daniels."

"Got it."

They headed for the main entrance of the dormitory and pushed through the double glass doors and into the foyer.

The corridors in both directions were empty, but Carson spotted a janitor's cart near a maintenance closet at the end of the hall on the left. "Come on."

He moved along the wide hallway carpeted in gray, with Ava next to him. He watched a man in his early fifties come out of a janitor's closet and stack a handful of rags on his cart.

"Excuse me, sir." He stopped and pulled his badge and photo ID out of his jacket pocket. "I'm FBI Special Agent Mike

Daniels and this is my partner Agent Mary Walker."

The janitor gazed at the photo ID and back up at Carson.

"We're here to have a look at Jerome Hinshaw's dorm room. The investigation into his disappearance has hit a wall, and we're hoping to get things moving again. Can you tell me where room 236 is?"

"Second floor. Up the stairs and take a right. Last room on the left."

The man turned back to his job, but paused for an instant. "Hinshaw was a nice kid, real nice kid. Smart. Year-round student."

"Is his roommate here?"

"Not sure. Most of the summer students have taken off for the fourth of July holiday."

"Thanks."

The janitor nodded and moved back into the closet.

Carson walked toward the stairway with his fingers mentally crossed and Ava right next to him. With any luck they'd get some information from the roommate. They needed to know what Hinshaw had been working on before he died.

"Here it is. Number 236. The local cops were probably all over this place after he disappeared." Carson raised his hand to knock, but the door opened on its own at that moment and he found himself staring at a punk kid with long shaggy hair and glasses, holding a duffel bag in his hand.

"Charles Preston?"

He tilted his head back and stared at both of them, drawing his lips into a tight line. "Cops?"

"FBI. I'm Agent Daniels, this is Agent Walker. We'd like a minute of your time."

"Can't." He attempted to step out into the hall, but Carson blocked his exit. He didn't want to play bully, but there was too much riding on the answers stashed inside the college kid's head, and he didn't plan on leaving without them.

"Look, Charles. The leads on your buddy's disappearance have dried up like the Sahara. We just need a few minutes to try and snag some leads, then you're out of here."

Charles Preston took a step back and opened the door wide.

Carson felt relief as he stepped into the dorm room behind Charles.

"It's a good thing you aren't cops...I mean, local cops. I hate those pushy pigs."

Charles dropped his duffel bag onto one of the two beds in the room and turned around, placing his hands on his hips in a gesture of protest. "They came in here right after Jerome went missing and tore the place apart. Took his computer, his writings and anything else the hell they thought they could. They even took some of my things. I tried to stop them, but they threatened to arrest me."

Carson tried to gauge the young man's state of mind as he studied him in the shallow lighting of the overly tidy room that should have been littered with smelly socks and fast-food wrappers. An angle of persuasion solidified in his mind.

"Those local boys were out of line. They had no right to invade your space and not return your things after they processed the scene."

Charles Preston began to nod his head.

"I'm glad you're following me, Agent Daniels. Maybe you can talk to them. Make them give my stuff back."

"I'll see what I can do, but I'm going to need some help from you, as well."

Charles nodded. Their conspiratorial link had been firmly established, judging by the tight smile that pulled at his mouth. "They didn't get everything."

A thread of hope ran through Carson. He studied Charles. "Good. You got the jump on them."

"I borrowed Jerome's travel drive the day before he disappeared, and I forgot to give it back. I left it in the biology lab by accident. Good thing, because when I got back here they were ripping the place apart."

Carson picked his words carefully. Charles was becoming more agitated the more he discussed the injustice he felt had been perpetrated by the local police. It was time to reel him in.

"I'm sorry, man. If you let me have the information on the travel drive, I'll make sure they come out of this looking like a bunch of hooligans."

Charles was already moving to a desk in the corner, where he pulled open the top drawer and took out a flash drive attached to a neck strap. "Take it. I don't want it back. I just want my stuff."

"You got it." Carson reached out and didn't relax until he clutched the memory stick in his hand. "Thanks, Charles."

"I gotta go. My plane leaves in an hour and my folks are waiting for me."

"I understand." Carson gave Ava a nod toward the door and followed her out into the hallway.

Charles Preston closed the door and shuffled down the corridor without another word.

Ava dared to take a breath. She wasn't very good at deception, she decided as she followed Carson down the hall, down the stairs and out into the fading afternoon sun. The change in lighting caused her to shield her eyes as she waited for them to adjust.

Carson moved along the sidewalk in front of her, silhouetted against the dropping sun.

Her heart rate picked up as she stared at him, dressed in a suit and tie. The image made a shred of memory pop into her head, a snippet of recall that left her hopeful. She'd seen him dressed like this before. She knew it as well as she knew her own name.

"When we worked detail together you wore that suit."

He pulled up short. "Yeah. Did you remember something?"

"It's more like déjà vu."

"It's a start." He touched her hand for an instant, sending a surge of heat up her arm.

Carson walked toward the car, feeling a measure of satisfaction. With any luck they'd have their first real lead when he uploaded the information to his team.

The last of the sun had slipped away and evening was settling over the campus.

He watched Ava move around to the passenger door and his blood warmed. He studied the set of her shoulders, the calmness in her face. She was relaxed for the first time since he'd secured her from the cabin two and a half days ago. Anticipation crawled along his nerves.

It was too late to drive back to McLean. They needed to secure another vehicle before morning, when the car they were driving would be reported stolen.

"You did great in there," he said.

She looked up over the roof of the car. "I hope so. Jerome Hinshaw was a smart kid. He had his whole life in front of him. It's too bad he's dead."

A glimpse of sorrow passed over her features. She popped the door latch. "Are we driving back tonight?"

"No. I thought we'd get some dinner and a room, then see what kind of fireworks display Cambridge has to offer."

A smile spread on her lips, lips he wanted in the worst way to kiss.

"I like it. I'm feeling pretty exhausted... and hungry."

"Come on. Let's get out of here and take care of your needs. Red meat?"

She grinned and climbed into the car. "Oh, yeah. Maybe we're having a future NFL star who's working on muscle mass in utero."

Carson's heart rate picked up as her joke echoed inside his brain, driving home in concrete terms the fact that she carried his child. "How do you know he's not a she, planning to become a ballerina?"

She gazed over at him, an odd look of worry on her face that pulled her brows together. "I don't. I just want to get him or her into the world. Safe and healthy."

His stomach knotted as he reached over and cupped her cheek, feeling heat course through him where they made contact. A mix of desire and frustration ignited every nerve in his body, making him tense all over.

"I'll do whatever I have to do to protect you both."

"I believe you," she whispered, dropping her gaze.

Had he seen trust in her eyes for a brief second? Or was it simple gratitude? He wasn't sure. He only knew that when his child came into the world, he needed to be there in spite of what might be hiding in his DNA.

AVA WATCHED Carson pull back the drape a fraction and look out the motel window into the parking lot below. It was the third time in ten minutes, and it was starting to unravel the hours of stressless existence she'd enjoyed since dinner and the glitzy fireworks display they'd watched light up the skies over Cambridge.

"Still nothing?" she asked, amused when he pulled back from the window and glared at her a moment before plopping into a chair and grabbing a newspaper off the small round table in front of the window.

"It's a damn good thing." He stared at her over the top of the newsprint before slapping it back on the table and standing up again.

"What's wrong?" She pushed herself up off the bed, where she'd been lying on her side with her head propped on her hand. "If it'll make you feel better, let's go. I wouldn't mind driving. Besides, you're like a tiger in a cage right now. Why don't you try to relax?"

He stopped long enough to study her before he turned back to the window and reached for the drape again, only to stop himself before he took another look.

"Something's bothering me," he said, moving toward her. He took a seat on the bed across from hers. "How is it that you can recall seeing Jerome Hinshaw in the back of the limo, but no one else?"

"I don't know. It was darkish. But you're right. I should've been able to see the others in the car."

"Unless..." He leaned toward her. "Unless they knew you'd be able to identify them. That's why a chunk of your memory was altered. They used you as a mule with the intention of having you transport the chip to Russia, where someone on the other end would have removed it from your back, possibly without you even knowing what had transpired stateside."

"That's a scary thought. A mind snatcher. Who inside the CIA has talent like that?"

Carson considered her question. Dr. Resnick had that kind of training and talent. In fact, he'd spearheaded the agency's research into mind and thought alteration, but he'd retired six years ago and moved to Seattle. There had to be someone on this end who'd messed with Ava before she got on the airplane. More than likely it had happened in the back of the limo.

"Give it a rest. Get some sleep. This will

all still be here in the morning." She stood up and moved in next to him.

Her proximity raised the heat in his blood. "You're right. How's the ankle?"

She sat down next to him and raised her pant leg up past her knee before she put her foot up on the opposite bed. "Good. The swelling is down and I can walk on it without pain. I think I'll take off the bandage for a while."

He stared at her slender calf as she looped the Ace wrap around and around until her leg was bare.

Carson clamped his teeth together, fighting a wave of lust so intense it almost made him groan.

He stood up. The temperature in his blood rose higher. He wanted her with an intensity that threatened to consume him in a blaze he couldn't extinguish.

"What is it?" She jumped to her feet next to him. He could hear the worry in her voice, feel the tension build in the air around them.

"It's nothing…I just need to move."

Her hand on his arm sent a jolt of electricity into his body. He turned to her, still fighting his need, but losing the battle.

Ava stared at Carson, lost in a moment that seemed to tie them together in an inescapable knot. She was aware of her hand on his arm, of the feel of his skin under her fingertips.

Heat flooded her face and burned into her cheeks, marking her embarrassment, but she couldn't look away.

She memorized every detail—his blue eyes, straight nose, square jaw—until her gaze settled on his mouth.

In a rush of powerful emotion she leaned into him, grateful when he didn't resist.

Did he feel it, too? Was his desire as overwhelming as hers?

The answer came as he reached for her chin and tilted her face up.

Carson couldn't hold back the flood that raged through his veins. He brushed her lips with his, tasting the sweetness of her mouth as he pulled her against him.

She was his mission. Every inch of her body his territory to explore.

He ended the kiss, staring into her eyes,

now bright with anticipation. "Are you sure?" he asked, knowing he could never go back once he started.

She nodded and slipped out of his arms, fingering the buttons of her blouse.

A groan rose in his throat as he eased himself onto the bed, unable to take his eyes off her as she reached the last button, undid it and slid the blouse off.

He wanted to devour her again, as he had the first time they'd made love, but he held back, enjoying the burn as it consumed his patience.

Reaching out, he unbuttoned her pants and pulled the zipper down. Slipping his hands around onto her backside, he shoved her pants over her hips. They pooled around her feet. She stepped out of them and he stared up at her, taking her hands in his.

Tiny beads of sweat dotted her upper lip and shone in the low light coming from the bedside lamp.

Carson swallowed, trying to bring his raging desire into line long enough to take her gently.

"You're beautiful," he whispered.

She gave him a seductive half smile that worked only to drive him further from control.

He let go of her and came to his feet, undoing the buttons of his shirt, then the button and zipper of his slacks.

Ava couldn't take her eyes off Carson as he peeled off his shirt. The hard lines of his chest, bare and rippled with muscle, made her breath catch in her throat. She didn't dare look down. She already knew every inch of Carson Nash was as good or better than the last.

She closed her eyes, listening to his clothing being kicked off. To the sound of his desire-laden breath.

She'd been with him before, hadn't she? Hadn't she already felt his brand of desire on her body? She grasped at a tangle of faded memories that infused her with unspoken certainty.

Then his hands were on her. She didn't resist as he reached around to unhook her bra clasp. He pulled it off like an unwanted entanglement.

She opened her eyes as he ran his hand

from the nape of her neck down to just below her waist, catching her panties in his grasp.

A sigh escaped her as he freed her from the last impediment between them and ecstasy.

He pulled her against him, the heat of his desire burning against her abdomen.

She shivered and smiled as she raised her gaze to his.

His eyes darkened with desire, the intensity in his gaze raw and sensual.

Primal fires erupted inside her, pooling low in her belly. She was a goner as he pulled back the covers and lowered her to the cool sheets.

War raged in the back of Carson's mind as he devoured Ava's body. She was soft to the touch, sweet heaven to be enjoyed in slow, savory increments. But the beast inside him clawed to get out, venting heat through him like a volcanic eruption.

He tuned in to the feel of her. Focused on the friction generating in every place they made contact.

Holding back his desire to take her now,

he dropped kisses across the top of her shoulder, worked across her upper chest, finally ending the trail at her breast, where he took her nipple into his mouth.

Tasting, teasing, he flicked his tongue across it, eliciting a moan from deep in her throat.

His desire cranked up until he thought he'd explode. Rising, he stared down at the seductive smile on her perfect mouth.

Her eyes were bright, pleading. He watched her swallow and slide her tongue over her lips. His patience imploded.

The need in Ava's body rose to a level beyond extreme. If Carson didn't end her agony soon, she'd have no choice but to take over.

She opened for him, watching his pulse pound in his neck as he moved between her legs, crushing her to the bed.

A moan rumbled in her throat as he entered her, his need swollen and hot. With each powerful thrust, pleasure invaded her body.

She raised her hips to him, giving him access to the need inside her begging for satisfaction.

Carson's body responded to the raw pleasure that pounded his control to dust. Again and again he thrust, feeling her climax rise out of the heated rhythm between them.

He gritted his teeth, holding back for her.

Lowering his mouth to her neck, he nibbled her skin with his teeth, riding the line between agony and ecstasy until he brought her to orgasm underneath him. She squeezed around him.

White-hot heat seared his body. He found release and followed her into the frenzy, a guttural moan in his throat.

He spilled into her, riding the climactic wave until his body began to cool.

Going still, he gazed down at her and kissed the sensual swell of her lips, lingering over the feel of her beneath him.

"Bring back any memories?" he asked, watching her smile.

"No, but it created a new one."

"Good." He knew how to pleasure a woman and satisfy his own needs, but it had always been little more than a physical act to him.

Until now.

His emotions twisted as he closed his eyes for an instant. Ava was different, and no amount of training or emotional deprivation had taught him how to deal with that.

Chapter Twelve

Carson lay in the darkness with his eyes closed, listening to the sounds of the night.

The feel of Ava's body next to him gave him pause. He ran his hand over her lower abdomen. Hesitating, he spread his fingers out over the baby bump on her belly, the physical confirmation that they were indeed going to have a child.

He forced away an assault of emotions he'd never believed he'd have to tackle. He was a sworn bachelor. A warrior, too involved with his missions to see into the future, too preoccupied with his past to move forward.

He should have resisted his body's primal needs, but making love to her again had eclipsed their first encounter, and he instinctively knew he could never step back from her again.

Somewhere outside the motel room a car door closed. Carson opened his eyes, a measure of caution rising in his system. He glanced at the digital alarm clock on the bedside table: 4:00 a.m.

Easing away from her, he sat up and searched the floor next to the bed for his clothes.

Finding his pants, he pulled them on and stepped to the window. He pushed the drape aside and stared down into the parking lot below.

On the far side was a car with its dome light on. He could just make out the shadow of someone sitting in the passenger seat.

He noted the make and model—dark blue sedan. Could be an Agency ride. Concern wrapped around his insides.

A man walked across the parking lot toward the vehicle and a woman climbed out of the passenger side, meeting him at the rear of the car. He slipped his key into the trunk and opened it. Together they each took out a suitcase.

Late arrivals.

Carson tried to relax, but couldn't. He scanned the parking lot, studying the other vehicles in the lot, until his gaze settled on a car parked near the edge, partially shielded by a tree. That's when he saw it—the glow of a cigarette as the occupant of the car took a drag.

"Ava. Wake up. We've got to go."

She rolled over and groaned.

He stepped back from the window. "Come on, sweetheart. We've got trouble."

He reached the bed, picking up her clothes as he went.

The word *trouble* brought her to attention. She scrambled out of bed, snagging her clothes from him as she did. "How?"

"Don't know, but we've got to clear out before they locate us."

Carson grabbed his backpack and stuffed everything inside. He pulled on his shirt, strapped on his ankle holster and shoved his feet into his shoes.

Ava was dressed and ready to leave by the time he turned back to her.

"Lay the pillows out and cover them. It might buy us time." They shaped the pillows to look like sleeping people and covered them up, meeting next to the exit.

Carson turned the knob and pulled the door open. Leaning out, he shot a glance to the left along the walkway.

"Come on," he whispered, taking her hand. He held the knob as the door closed, keeping it silent.

They moved along the walkway without a sound, listening to the echo of footfalls coming up the open-air stairway at the end of the complex.

The agents had no doubt gotten the room number from the motel manager. They were seconds away from detection. If not for the late arrivals, Carson and Ava would've been sitting ducks.

At the last minute they stepped into a tiny room housing an ice machine.

Carson pulled her against the wall next to him, listening to the footsteps headed in their direction.

The sound of two male voices rose above the hum of the ice-machine compressor.

He strained to hear their conversation as their voices gradually became clear.

"A couple matching their description is in room 212. That's up here at the end of the line."

Ava held her breath and closed her eyes, trying to blend in to the wall next to Carson. From ecstasy to terror all in one night was more than she could handle, but she remained frozen in place, listening to certain death move closer with each passing second.

Her pulse thumped. Only the feel of Carson next to her offered hope.

"You match the plate number on their car?"

"Yeah. It's in the parking lot. Jensen did the tail outside Hinshaw's place. Nash has been declared a rogue. It'll make killing him and his package less of a stretch."

"Cozy."

Rage built in Carson as he listened to the agents talk as they moved past their hiding place. Someone had betrayed their decision to check out Hinshaw. There was only one person he'd told, and he was three thousand miles away.

"This is it." The men were approximately seven doors down.

Carson heard the double beep of the key card in the door and took Ava's hand.

The click of the handle was his cue. He stepped into the doorway and glanced to the right just as the men entered the motel room.

"Let's go." He timed their exit with the closing of the door.

"Don't look back," he instructed as they covered the distance to the stairway.

They hit the end of the walkway and raced down the stairs. Carson pulled up short at the bottom of the landing. He'd parked the car directly under the window of the room so he could keep an eye on it, but that meant the agents upstairs had only to look out to see their escape, and their lookout driver would spot them the minute they emerged from the shadows.

It was a risk they'd have to take.

He pulled the key out of his pocket, staring down into her face cast in shadow from the streetlights.

"Keep your head down and don't stop moving." He didn't have the heart to tell her the CIA's net was closing much faster than he'd ever anticipated.

Taking her hand, he led her along the sidewalk.

Keeping his focus on the car, he didn't look up until he'd opened the passenger door and Ava was safe inside.

The drape slapped shut in their vacant room.

They'd been made.

Carson skirted the car and jumped in. He shoved the key into the ignition and fired the engine.

"Hang on!" He put the car in Reverse and backed out of the space, slipped it into Drive and cranked the wheel, tromping on the gas pedal. The car shot forward. He braked for a second and whipped out onto the street, headed south.

"Where are we going?"

"To ditch this car. The plates have been made. We're sitting targets if we don't get rid of it."

"So we're walking back to McLean?"

He liked her sense of humor, but he couldn't muster a comeback. "No way." He glanced up into the rearview mirror. The road behind them was clear. He sped up, hoping to widen the gap for the time being.

He braked for an instant and took the corner. The tires squealed and the suspension buckled. He feathered the brakes and kept it on the road.

"Find me a place where the Charles River bends with a road next to it." It was risky, but they needed to get away clean. Ava fumbled in the glove box for the map of Cambridge they'd used to find the MIT campus. She pulled it out and turned on the dome light.

Studying the map, she spotted a place that matched his description. "Soldiers Field Road. We can access it from Western Avenue. The street we used this afternoon."

"Got it." Carson slowed the car.

Panicking, Ava turned in the seat and looked behind them. "What are you doing? They'll catch up with us."

"Yeah. Now tell me what the road looks like after we get onto it."

Confusion fed her fear, growing disproportionately to his calm demeanor.

She'd have to trust him. Trust that he

knew what he was doing. She stared at the map and gave him directions to the river, then added, "But the road is a narrow two-way."

"Don't sweat it." He glanced up into the rearview mirror. "Here they come."

Turning, she watched in horror as a dark sedan fell in behind them approximately half a mile back and closing.

She stomped her foot against the floor-board several times in frustration, pressing an imaginary gas pedal that could jettison them out of reach, but it was futile.

"Relax. Everything's under control."

"Whose control?" Her nerves were frazzled, but she wanted more than anything to understand his madness.

"We're going to launch this car into the Charles River. But," he qualified, "we'll be high and dry. They'll spend hours trying to fish our bodies out of the water to retrieve the microchip. By then we'll be a quarter of the way back to McLean."

For the first time since leaving the motel room in a panic, she relaxed. Carson was a capable man. A man she could count on.

"A bus?"

"Any way we can get there. I saw an umbrella on the floorboard of the backseat. Grab it for me."

She undid her seat belt and leaned over, retrieving the black bag. Turning around, she buckled back into her seat and pulled the umbrella out of its cover. Glancing up, she looked down into the black water as they sailed over the Western Avenue bridge.

They were minutes from their final turn, a thought that set her nerves on edge.

"I'm going to stop along the road up ahead. I want you to get out of the car and hide in the ditch. No matter what happens, don't move until I come for you."

She stared over at Carson, afraid for him, but he laid his hand on her leg and she felt his strength infuse her body.

"We have a child to raise."

Emotions, charged and poignant, closed her throat as she stared ahead, watching as a stop sign loomed in front of them. *We?* The word made hope churn in her mind—hope that she wouldn't have to raise her child alone without a father.

Carson stomped on the brake, glanced to the left and slid around the corner onto Soldiers Field Road.

Raising his eyes to the mirror, he watched the headlights of the chase car make the corner less than a quarter of a mile behind them.

The timing would have to be perfect— he'd calculated the maneuver down to the last component. There was only one element that could make this fail.

"Promise me you'll do exactly what I said." He glanced at Ava, a silent prayer on his lips for her safety and the safety of their baby.

"Piece of cake. Just stay safe."

Silence dogged the interior of the car. He had to give her credit for knowing how risky the maneuver was.

"What kind of closure does the umbrella have?"

"A two-stage push button. The first one opens the shaft, the next one the umbrella."

"Open the shaft and hand it to me."

He heard the shaft release with a tinny hiss. Reaching over with his right hand, he took it from her and lowered it until he felt it against the toe of his shoe. Rocking the handle back, he attempted to touch the bottom edge of the seat, but it was an inch short.

"I've got to adjust the seat, but it'll work." He laid the umbrella down next to him and fiddled with the seat controls, moving the seat forward. He needed to rig the gas pedal.

Up ahead in the headlights he could see the beginning of the turn. "This is it."

A knot twisted in his gut as he pressed down hard on the gas. The car shot forward, opening the distance between them and the carload of agents.

The trees whipped past the window as the turn sharpened, putting them out of view of the chase car.

Carson slammed on the brakes. The car slid to a stop. Ava opened the door and bailed out, darting into the tall grass next to the roadway.

Carson hit the gas pedal at the same time he reached for the umbrella.

He jammed it down on the accelerator, wedging it against the bottom of the seat.

The overrevved howl of the engine cut into his senses. He popped the door handle and grabbed his pack.

In the last second before launch, he pulled the steering wheel hard to the left as the corner veered right, and dived out of the moving car.

AVA LAY DEEP in the ditch hidden in the tall grass surrounding her.

The eerie sound of the car hitting the water a hundred yards away from her hiding spot put a ripple of terror in her blood.

Was Carson alive? Had he made it out before the violent plunge into the Charles River? Was he injured and lying in the middle of the road where the agents would find him and kill him for sure?

The chase car whizzed past, followed by the sound of squealing brakes.

She closed her eyes, repeating Carson's words over and over in her head. She was safe here. Safe as long as she didn't move, didn't cry out, didn't give up her location to men who would kill her if they found her. Whether she was dead or alive, they'd cut the microchip out of her body. She swallowed as the horrible image messed with her mind. Sucking in a breath, she redirected her thoughts, focusing instead on the memory of Carson lying next to her.

Carson gritted his teeth and lay still in the vegetation next to the road. He was banged up, but he'd live.

The screech of tires and slam of car doors gave away the enemy's position. Unfortunately it wasn't far enough away in his mind. He'd barely made it out of the car in time, and it put him precariously close to the three agents in the chase car.

"Dammit to hell. I hate the water."

"Jensen. You're going in. We only need the girl."

"How deep do you think it is?"

"Fifteen, maybe twenty feet."

"If we don't recover that microchip, we're dead. You know that, don't you?"

"What's Poltergeist got on you, anyway?"

"None of your damn business. What's he got on you?"

"If we don't pull together, it won't matter what he has on any of us. We're as good as dead. Now, find some damn rope so we can go in after the girl."

Tension froze every muscle in Carson's body as he peered through the low brush and grass he'd landed in on his belly. The first hint of dawn was beginning to lighten the sky overhead.

In less than an hour there'd be enough light to be seen.

He swallowed, watching the men open the trunk of the car and search around inside, finally pulling out a coil of rope.

"Fifty feet, that's it. It better be enough."

"Pull the car up as close as you can to the riverbank. Maybe we can spot the car with the headlights."

He tried to make out the identities of the three agents clustered around the car. The poor lighting didn't help, but he was sure he'd never seen any of them before tonight.

One of the men opened the driver's door and climbed into the car. The man behind the wheel rolled the window down and poked his head out, looking up and down the road.

The back-up lights came on as the car

rolled in his direction, stopping less than ten feet short of his position.

"Jensen, what the hell are you doing?"

"Looking for a spot closer to the riverbank."

"Try farther up the road. It's more level where they went in."

"The hell it is." The driver let off the brake. The car rolled closer.

Carson held his breath, ready for evasive maneuvers if the vehicle came close enough to run over him, but the driver applied the brakes again less than three feet away.

"Jensen!" someone bellowed from farther up the road.

The smell of car exhaust polluted Carson's lungs, but he didn't move. It would be suicide to choke.

He heard the car's transmission jolt into Drive, and pulled in a deep breath as the vehicle moved forward, stopping sixty feet up the road.

He reached down and pulled his gun out of its ankle holster in slow motion, tucking it under his chest.

Time was short. Within the hour the

agents would know the car was empty, and their window of escape would close.

The hair at his nape bristled at the same time he felt a boot slam into his back from behind.

"Son of a bitch. Look who we got here. The infamous Agent Carson Nash."

Chapter Thirteen

Carson's reaction to the threat was swift and deadly.

In half a second he twisted around, aimed his 9 mm and double tapped the man standing over him.

Rolling deep into the ditch, he watched the stunned agent drop.

He rose out of the grass, searching for the other two in the pale darkness. He caught signs of movement in his peripheral vision on the right.

Turning toward it, he stared over his gun sight at a couple of figures in the middle of the road.

Worry sliced into him, cutting loose his rage. He moved forward, out onto the pavement.

"Let her go," he demanded, just able to make out the expression of terror on Ava's face as the agent walked her forward, his arm around her waist from behind as he used her as a human shield.

"Put the gun down or she gets it." The man pushed the barrel of his gun against Ava's jaw, just under her chin.

Fear shot through Carson.

The rogue agent had nothing to lose.

"Okay…okay." He lowered his weapon, laying it on the ground next to his right foot. "Jensen! Get over here."

Behind him, Carson heard a car door open and slam shut, then footsteps on the asphalt.

Slowly he turned, determined to keep both men in sight and protect his back.

"Well, what do you know. She's not at the bottom of the Charles. I won't have to get wet after all."

The agent holding Ava grunted. "Let's get what we came for, drown them together and get the hell out of here. Daylight's coming."

Carson tensed, watching the agent reach into his pocket and pulled out a knife.

The blade snapped open and he moved in.

Fear twisted around Ava's heart as she stared at Carson in the predawn light. The feel of the gun barrel against her chin had rendered her thought processes null and void, but she had to think. Had to focus on the coming assault and her reaction to it, if she wanted to live.

Keeping her eyes on Carson, she tried to figure out what his next move might be. Glancing down, she watched him position his foot right next to his discarded gun. A marker of sorts, she decided as she watched the agent coming toward her with an open knife in his hand.

It would be up to her to create a clear shot for Carson. They'd have one chance before the knife blade found its way into her flesh.

She swallowed.

The agent with the knife moved in next to them. "Too bad Poltergeist chose such a nice piece of eye candy for a mule."

"Stop slobbering and get it done!" yelled the agent holding her.

A shudder twisted along her spine as he repositioned the gun and turned her toward him, exposing her back to the man with the blade.

Now.

With all the strength she could muster, she bent over and lunged forward, head-butting the agent in the gut.

She heard him grunt as he rocked back from the force.

Dodging right, she dived for the pavement, anticipating the impact.

In that split second Carson saw his opportunity.

He snagged his gun from the ground and charged forward.

Ava was clear.

Rage erupted in his bloodstream.

Agent Jensen whirled to face him.

Pop! Pop! He double tapped him in the forehead.

He dropped.

Carson set his sights on the other thug, who struggled to regain his balance, his gun still in his hand.

A shot went off, unmuffled and loud in the dawn air.

A bullet zinged past Carson's ear.

Pop! He took the shot before the agent could take aim again.

He dropped.

Relief spilled over him as he raced toward Ava, who'd pulled up into a sitting position in the middle of the road.

Carson kicked the agent's gun away before kneeling next to her. He pulled her into his arms, smoothing her hair away from her face. "Are you sure you don't want to join my team?"

"I'm a confirmed paper pusher—you know that." She gazed up at him.

"No pressure, but we need to get out of here before our luck takes a turn." He looked around at the carnage. "When these rogues don't report in, all hell's going to break loose."

"Looks like we found a ride." She motioned to the car as he helped her to her feet.

"Not exactly what I had in mind, but the appropriation of available assets applies in this case."

She looked up at him and smiled. "See, that's why I could never join your little band of merry men. You don't speak plain English. Translated—the car's here, we're taking it."

He liked her simple assessment of the situation and everything else about her, he decided as they loaded the dead agents into the trunk of the car and closed the lid.

Unfortunately, there was nothing simple about the trouble they were in. "You gave me the shot." He stared down at her, fighting the images of her body next to his.

"It was fight back or let that maniac carve into my skin." She shuddered.

He pulled her into his arms for an instant, sobered by how close he'd just come to losing her.

It was time to chop the head off the snake before they got bitten. He had to find Poltergeist, the man behind the microchip in Ava, and take him down any way he could.

CARSON HIT THE SEND BUTTON on the Cambridge Public Library's computer and sat back in his chair, eyeing Ava over the top of the monitor.

Jerome Hinshaw's files would be in his

team's hands for analysis. With any luck, they'd know in a couple of hours what information the microchip contained.

He pulled the flash drive out of the USB port and shut down the computer.

"I see hunger in your eyes, Agent Ross," he said as he stood up.

"Yeah. I'm thinking red meat."

"I'm not." He stared at her, watching a seductive smile turn her mouth. "You could drive a vegetarian to backslide with an appetite like that."

"Really?" Ava tried to bring her raging pulse under control, but the blistering heat in Carson's stare was so intense she felt her skin warm.

She was hungry. Hungry to feel him again. Hungry for the soul-seducing pleasure he'd heaped on her last night, but she wondered if she could ever understand a man like Carson Nash.

A man who was comfortable surrounded by danger. He took lives for a living, but he'd saved hers more than once. Where was the balance? Could they find it together?

"I'm not into sex in public places. I

prefer to satisfy my hunger in private, or at a great restaurant. You need to eat before we get on the road."

A measure of disappointment flooded her veins as she followed him out of the library and to the car they'd purchased through a private-party ad in the local newspaper, after ditching the agents' car.

She didn't even plan to ask where he'd gotten the licence plates he'd put on the vehicle, as long as they got back to the safety of the apartment ASAP.

Full of foreboding, she climbed into the car.

There were more agents just like the three they'd escaped and she couldn't help but feel they were heading blindfolded into a shooting gallery.

Resting her hand on her baby bump, she prayed Carson could find the answers in time to save them all.

CARSON WILLED the nagging questions in his head to be still, but it did no good. There was no doubt that their location in Cambridge had been compromised by someone he thought he could trust. The man lived three thousand miles away, but Dr. Resnick was the only one who knew they'd planned to go to Jerome Hinshaw's place in search of answers.

He straightened, alert, as the picture began to clear. If Resnick was behind Ava's memory loss, then he knew how to restore the loss, as well.

He glanced over at her as she slept, leaning against the side window in the car. They were almost home. Almost safe.

He gritted his teeth. Anger festered inside him. What kind of animal was Resnick anyway? He knew about the baby she was carrying, yet he'd given pertinent information to the three agents Carson had had to kill.

Everyone had a limit. Where was Resnick's?

Carson maneuvered through the city streets, finally turning into the parking garage of his building.

The tentacles of Resnick's operation could potentially wrap around a lot of other operatives. He'd spent a considerable amount of time in the CIA dealing with mind control research and experiments that defied human logic.

He pulled into a parking space and turned off the car.

Was Ava a ticking time bomb? Destined to go off at some point? He was familiar with the good doctor's work with assassins programmed to be turned on and off like switches. Devoid of thought outside their mission and virtually uncrackable during interrogations.

Reaching over, he stroked her hair, rousing her out of sleep. She startled awake, sitting bolt upright in the seat. "Where are we?"

"We're back at the apartment."

She visibly relaxed. "What time is it?"

"Almost seven."

The ring tone of his cell phone went off. Carson pulled the phone from his belt, checking the screen before answering. "What've you got?"

"You're not going to like this." The sound of Agent Nick Shelby's concerned voice come over the airwaves.

"Hinshaw's research?"

"The guy was working on some dangerous stuff, depending on whose side you're on."

Carson's gut tightened.

"The research files on the travel drive are incomplete. He religiously detailed his findings and diagrammed his prototypes, up until five months ago. Then it stops abruptly. We've all had a look at this and the consensus is he developed and produced a bootleg microchip."

"You're sure it went to production?"

"From what's here. Yeah."

Worry flooded his mind. "What's its function and capacity?"

"Spy satellite aiming and trajectory. The worst part is he was able to create a frequency that precisely matches the host nation's command center. The host country would have no idea another nation had commandeered their spy satellites until it was too late. They could launch an invisible strike."

"I'll be damned." Carson's mind was on fire with the realization. Ava had been used as a mule to transport the microchip to its buyer. Russia. Only she hadn't made the plane and now both parties in the deal were willing to kill her to get it back. One because they'd paid for it. The other because they couldn't risk discovery of the transaction. That explained the NSA's role, but were they the problem or the solution?

"Thanks, buddy."

"You know you don't have to tackle this monster by yourself. Just say the words."

The air between them was charged with anticipation as Carson considered his options.

"It could get dicey," he said, wanting the understanding in place before they even debated deployment.

"We're addicted to adrenaline. We eat dicey for lunch."

"The clock is ticking—it's a quarter to midnight." Carson said the go-code phrase into his cell phone and hung up.

He tried to tamp down the alarm that pulsed through his body. In an instant they'd become pawns in a matter of national security, but that wasn't the driving conflict in his head, or his worst concern.

It was the woman in the seat next to him and the child inside her. He had to find a way to save them both, even if it cost him his life.

AVA RAN HER FINGERTIPS over the contours of Carson's chest and watched a smile spread on his lips. There were nonphysical areas of him she'd yet to touch, but not from lack of trying. He was a man with secrets. Some she could live with—others she guessed had scared holes in him that needed filling.

And then there was the child she carried. Although he rarely asked questions, she'd felt the intensity of his emotions when he'd covered her abdomen with his hand to feel the growing baby inside her.

What was he afraid of? What inner battles did he fight?

Leaning over, she kissed him on the mouth. A surge of desire rocked her emotions into an avalanche of need she couldn't escape. It rolled her senses in a protective cocoon, enhanced by the feel of his arms as he moved her on top of him and pulled her closer.

Carson tried to tone down the raging lust that possessed his body every time he touched her, but it was useless, and he realized his mind had given up resistance long before his body had.

Reaching up, he stroked her hair back as he stared at her in the dim light filtering through the bedroom window. "How can I ever say no to you?"

A smile parted her lips as she leaned toward him. "Do you want to?"

Heat burned through him as she pushed back, brushing his shaft. "Dammit, woman."

In one swift movement he rolled her underneath him, hearing her shallow gasp as he thrust into her, barely able to restrain himself.

Heat sizzled through his body, lighting up every nerve ending.

Her soft moans of pleasure coaxed him deeper and deeper inside her. He felt her climax as she tightened around him, whispering his name.

White light exploded behind his eyelids. He tensed and relaxed as pleasure rocked his body.

Satiated, he nuzzled her neck, nibbling

slowly across the ridge of her shoulder. Every time with her was better than the time before, a fact that did little to alleviate his troubles. Where was his control? His grit? The same restraint that had pushed him to the top of his command and beyond.

He'd relinquish it, all of it, just to know Ava and the baby would be safe.

"If I weren't already pregnant, that would have done it," she whispered, gazing up at him with a sweet smile on her mouth.

He stared down at her, swallowing against the knot of emotion in his chest. She knew nothing about his past. Nothing of the vow he'd made after watching his father nearly kill his mother for the last time.

Could he ever be good enough for her? Could he alter his DNA so history didn't repeat itself?

"I'll do what's right for you and the baby. You know that, don't you?"

Her smile faded and he saw a sparkle of moisture in her eyes. "I can't force you to be a part of our child's life if you don't want to be. I've made my peace with the idea of single parenthood."

Carson's heart twisted as he tried to imagine life without her, or his child.

"There are things you don't know about me, about my upbringing."

"So you've got childhood issues. Who doesn't? It can't be that bad."

He'd never been one to spill his guts, and he hadn't planned to start tonight, but somehow she'd managed to dig into his soul, and she deserved to know the truth.

"My father was military. A drill sergeant. Strict as hell. If he said jump, you jumped. But he didn't only behave this way toward his men—he brought it home at night." Carson's throat tightened. Reaching up, he rubbed the deep scar above his left eyebrow—a physical reminder of their last encounter.

She would hate him, mistrust him when he was finished. But he couldn't let her believe he'd be an ideal father for their child, not when he didn't trust his own genetics.

"When I was fourteen, he almost beat my mother to death. If I hadn't stepped in, he would have killed her that night."

"Is that where you got this?"

The feel of her fingertips rubbing the scar soothed his nerves and infused him with the courage to go on.

"Yeah. My mother divorced the SOB two years after. He died more than ten years ago, never having voiced regret for the things he did to us. My mom told me after his death that he'd grown up in a violent home. That his father had beaten him and his mother for years. So the pattern continues through generations—"

"Until someone with courage and strength comes forward to stop it." Ava's heart squeezed in her chest. "You're not your father, or your grandfather. The cycle can be broken."

He stared down at her. A muscle worked along his jawline, his features unreadable in the low light.

"Genetics can't be altered." Slowly he moved off her and rolled onto his side.

She turned to face him, trying to get a sense of where he was emotionally, but she couldn't.

Did he really believe what he was saying? Had the tragedies of the past trapped the knowledge so deep in his psyche he'd never be able to root it out?

Worry skittered over her thoughts as she closed her eyes and reached out to touch him, hoping she could change his mind somehow.

SLEEP ELUDED CARSON like the winning Powerball numbers.

Giving up, he crawled out of bed, leaving Ava snuggled under the covers, a slight smile on her mouth highlighted in the dim glow of the alarm clock on the bedside table.

It was 2:13 a.m.

Tension gripped his body as he pulled on his boxers and strode out of the bedroom, closing the door behind him.

What had happened to his mental guard? He'd spilled his guts to her like a double agent to his foreign handler once he'd crossed the border.

He went into the kitchen and got a glass of water. Leaning against the counter, he tried to get a handle on his emotions.

He couldn't imagine not having her with him, in his life, in his bed, but it didn't make him happy—it only added to the growing concern racing through his mind.

They were a long way from commitment. And he was further still from assimilating the fragments of tenderness that churned inside him. Tenderness could spell death in his line of work.

His cell phone went off in the darkness.

Carson picked his way around the furniture and snagged the phone off its charger.

"Hello."

"You've got to get out!"

He recognized the sound of Gary Resnick's voice on the other end of the line.

"You SOB. You sold us out."

The airwaves fuzzed with white noise, sputtered and cleared again.

"Your location has been compromised!"

A shout rose over the line as another man's voice interrupted Resnick's warning.

"Resnick! Resnick!" Carson tried to reestablish the connection over the sound of a scuffle taking place three thousand miles away.

"Kak tvoyo zdorovie sevodn'a!" Resnick yelled.

Carson grasped the words of the phrase spoken in Russian.

"What does it mean!"

Pop! Pop!

Gunfire exploded on the other end of the connection.

Chapter Fourteen

The line went dead in Carson's hand.

He closed the phone, his heart hammering in his eardrums.

Was Resnick really trying to warn them? Or was it a ruse to draw them out into the open so they could be picked off by Poltergeist and his rogues?

The sound of the bedroom door opening caught him off guard.

Ava stepped into the doorway, visible in the light from the street lamps that filtered through the covered windows of the apartment.

"Is everything okay? I heard shouting."

He stared at her, caught up in indecision. Maybe he should heed Resnick's warning and run like hell. But what if he was wrong?

"That was Dr. Resnick in Seattle. He claims this safe house has been compromised."

Ava moved toward him. He could see worry on her face. Her brows pulled together as he watched her. "We have to go. If they catch us here—"

"They're not going to." He grasped her by the upper arms. "He said something in Russian. Maybe you know what it means."

"Tell me."

Carson repeated the Russian phrase, hoping he'd said it correctly.

"How's your health today?" Ava translated.

Carson felt her sway, but caught her before she collapsed. Moving her to the couch, he sat down next to her.

Worried, he stared into her face.

Ava's mind was spinning. Something in the words he'd spoken were mining deep in her gray matter, burrowing past and under the walls that blocked her memories. She tried to speak, but her tongue wouldn't respond.

She closed her eyes. Unfamiliar images flashed in her head, along with snippets of dialogue as memories of the past four months collided in her brain.

Her stomach churned.

She opened her eyes, sat forward and saw Carson for what seemed like the first time. Her heart rate cranked up. She stood. "My memory's coming back." She sucked in a breath and closed her eyes.

He came to his feet beside her. "The limo, Ava. Who was in the limo?"

Frustration rippled through her as she worked to force the answer out.

"Take your time. It'll come."

She did as he said, feeling calm settle over her agitated senses. "The car came to pick me up. I can see the driver climb out. He's coming around to open the door for me. I looked up at the bedroom window." Heat flashed through her as the vivid memory of the first night she'd spent in Carson's arms blazed in her mind.

"He opened the door, and I climbed in. It's hard to see…Jerome Hinshaw is there, on the seat next to Dr. Resnick." Ava's eyes flew open. She stared at Carson. "Resnick was there. I didn't know who he was at the time."

"Who else is in the car?"

Again she closed her eyes, moving through the events of that morning.

Terror, chilling and infinite, skittered along her spine as the identity of the last occupant of the car came into focus.

"Director Glendow…my boss. He killed Jerome Hinshaw when he refused to turn over the microchip without getting his money. He stabbed him to death in the backseat."

Shocked, Carson digested Ava's revelation.

Director Glendow was behind Hinshaw's murder, and he was desperate to recover the lost chip.

Dr. Resnick had blocked the memory of the murder and implantation from Ava's mind, but he'd left a back door into her repressed recall, accessible with a Russian phrase known only to him.

"Don't turn on the lights. Get dressed. Resnick didn't trust Glendow. If he had he'd never have left a recall phrase in place."

Carson's nerves stretched tight as he dressed and gathered his survival gear.

Ava was right next to him as he pulled the curtain aside and stared out at the grounds below shrouded in shadow. It was a limited view, something that put a knot in his gut.

Entering the parking garage would be risky. There was no way to see the enemy coming.

He let the drape go and stepped back. "Put on my extra vest."

"Okay." She swallowed and went pale.

"Promise me you won't take it off until this is over."

"I promise."

He brushed a lock of hair behind her ear with his hand and raised her chin, intent on alleviating the fear in her eyes. "I won't let anything happen to you."

"I know," she whispered, brushing her hand against his.

Carson fought an overwhelming desire to kiss her. "We've got to move. They're probably watching, planning to take us the moment we step out of this apartment." He pulled his pistol out of its holster and checked his rounds. It would serve them better to elude than to stand and fight. He couldn't risk running Ava through a hail of bullets.

He looked at his watch. It was almost 3:00 a.m.

"Sit tight." He watched her slide into a dining-room chair.

Carson laid the gun down and fished in his pack, taking out his minicamera. He walked to the apartment door and went to his knees. Stretching out on the floor, he pulled loose the tiny flap of threshold rubber he'd altered months ago when he'd been given the high-tech gadget.

He turned on the switch at the base of the instrument and pushed the end, no bigger around than a pencil, into the gap in the rubber.

Carson lowered his head and gazed through the minilens connected to a 360-degree fish-eye camera that protruded into the hallway outside the apartment door, giving him a view of the entire area in both directions.

He looked into the viewfinder, scanning for movement outside in the corridor. It was clear, but he couldn't calm his feeling of foreboding.

Could they risk a run for the car and escape? Or would Glendow's rogue agents stop them before they could even start? He couldn't risk their lives on it.

He pulled the instrument out of the hole and shut it off. Standing, he moved to the table and picked up his pistol.

"Whatever happens, stay here. I'm going to check the stairwell." He paused. "I'm serious, Ava. Stay here."

Ava nodded, watching him move to the door. He opened it and poked his head out before disappearing into the hallway.

She stood up, unable to relax as she paced the apartment.

Drawing in a deep breath, she paused, sniffing the acrid scent in the air around her.

Panic seized her as she pulled in another breath laced with the smell of smoke.

The building was on fire.

Ava bolted for the window and pulled back the drape.

A veil of black smoke roiled past the window, coming from the apartment directly underneath Carson's.

The sound of breaking glass put her on

edge. It was followed by the scream of a fire alarm sending its warning to all corners of the complex.

Carson slipped back inside the door and closed it behind him.

"Get ready to run. They've torched the second floor."

He moved to the table, snagged his backpack and put the camera device inside before he zipped it closed. He shoved his pistol into the back of his waistband.

"The hallway is filling up. Let's go."

He took her hand as they left the apartment, merging with other residents anxious to escape the smoke now wisping its way up to the third floor.

Over the tops of bobbing heads, Carson kept his eye on the end of the hallway where the stairwell door exited to the floors below.

The door opened, revealing a man dressed in jeans and a T-shirt, but his casual dress didn't conceal his identity. Carson had seen him before—in Seattle, outside Resnick's house, with a knife to Ava's back.

Carson slowed his pace and allowed the

others to filter past them until they were at the back of the mass exodus.

"One of Glendow's men is guarding the exit. Stay behind me until I give the order to move."

He released her hand and nudged her in behind him. Picking up his pace, he bellied up to the people in front of him, using them as cover.

He watched the agent glance up, scanning faces as they funneled into the stairwell.

Tension wound around his nerves. He'd have one chance to take the man out without raising the alarm.

Carson closed his right hand into a fist, visualizing his tactical move as the last of the residents filtered into the stairwell in front of him.

The agent looked up.

They made eye contact for an instant.

Carson lunged forward, jammed his left forearm against the agent's throat and pinned him to the stairwell door.

He shoved the man to the left.

The door he'd been holding open slammed shut.

"Move, Ava!"

In his peripheral vision he saw her lunge for the stairwell door.

The elevator chime sounded. The doors ground open.

Carson glanced up, a guttural yell lodged in his throat.

An agent rushed out of the carriage and grabbed Ava. He locked his arm around her waist and dragged her across the threshold and into the elevator.

Carson raised his fist and punched his captive right between the eyes, dropping him like a rock.

He pulled the gun out of his waistband and rushed forward, leveling the sights on the man's forehead, but he hesitated.

Ava was too close.

Rage fired inside him.

The elevator doors began to close.

Charging forward, he ignored the man's raised gun, barely flinching as a silenced double tap slammed into his chest.

In a desperate attempt to save her, he squeezed through the narrow gap in the doors and crashed into the pair.

The impact sent Ava sprawling, knocking the wind out of her as she clawed her way into the corner of the cubicle.

Carson landed blow after blow on the agent, but he wouldn't surrender.

Terror coated her insides. She looked down, spotting Carson's gun on the floor at the same time as she saw the gleam of a knife blade in the opposing agent's hand.

She rocked forward and grabbed the pistol.

Taking aim, she pulled the trigger once.

A cry of pain pierced her ears.

The agent stumbled back, a gaping wound in his thigh.

Carson punched him, completing the knockdown. Reaching down, he pulled the agent's gun out of his hand and straightened.

He stared at Ava, sitting in the corner. Stepping over the man, he pulled her to her feet just as the carriage stopped on the garage level.

"I've never had to shoot anyone before." She stared at him, concern in her eyes.

A measure of sympathy moved through

him. He brushed her cheek with his fingers. "With any luck you'll never have to do it again, but you have to remember, it's kill or be killed by these guys. They want one thing—you and the chip you're carrying. They made their choice. Don't hesitate to make yours if your life is threatened. Trade you. Take this one—you might need it."

She gave him a resigned nod as he handed her the agent's pistol and she gave him the 9 mm.

Carson held the doors with his hand, moving Ava in next to him.

He leaned forward, surveying the garage from the safety of the carriage.

Reaching into his pocket, he pulled out the car keys. "You drive. I'll take shotgun." She took the keys from him, brushing his skin in the handoff. A jolt of heat sizzled up his arm, but he extinguished it, perplexed by his body's reaction to even the smallest of her touches.

Determination flooded his body as he refocused his thoughts on the car and escape.

"Stay low. Follow me."

"Got it."

Hunched down, Carson bolted out of the elevator, with Ava right behind him.

The parking structure echoed with sirens that covered any other sounds going on around them.

Carson ducked in behind a pickup truck.

In commando fashion, he picked out their next cover and skittered to it.

Ava followed right behind him, her nerves on edge. Cover was great, but they could be picked off any time. Staring around the back quarter panel of the truck, she spotted the car and squeezed the key in her hand.

Somewhere behind her she heard the sound of footsteps pounding the concrete.

Wheeling toward the sound, she watched as a man took cover behind a car less than fifty feet away. "They're behind us, Carson!"

Panic filled her, and she clutched the pistol in her hand.

"We're almost there. I'll provide cover— you get the car."

She had to trust him. Had to allow his expertise to dominate the mission. "What about the guy behind us?"

"Leave him to me." Carson maneuvered Ava in front of him.

"Go-go-go!"

He whirled around just as the agent behind them stepped out from his cover and charged forward.

Taking aim, Carson squeezed off a shot, nailing him in the chest, but the man kept coming.

Firing again, he caught him in the leg. He went down.

Carson bolted for the car right behind Ava.

She jumped in and fired up the engine.

"Let's get out of here!"

She popped the car into Reverse and zipped backward, braked and put the car into Drive.

A bullet hit the back windshield, shattering the tempered glass into a million pieces.

"Drive!" he ordered.

Carson turned in the seat and returned fire as Ava sped through the parking garage and out the exit.

She zigzagged through a smattering of arriving fire trucks and EMS vehicles, and pulled out onto the main drag.

A dark sedan pulled away from the curb shortly after they passed and fell in behind them, keeping its distance.

"We've got company. We need to take him out before he can call in reinforcements."

Ava stepped down on the gas pedal and glanced into the rearview mirror at the headlights less than an eighth of a mile back. Her nerves were in shreds. "You know I got my driver's licence out of a cereal box." She swallowed the lump of fear in her throat.

"Can't take the heat?"

She glared at him for an instant before refocusing on the road in front of her.

"Tell you what. I'll drive if you want to shoot."

She hated the sound of that even more. "Where to?"

"The nearest stoplight. Reel him in so I can take him out."

Fear laced through her as she stared down the road at the intersection coming up. The light was green.

Shifting the transmission into Low, she felt the car jolt before the engine's rpms came down and the speedometer needle dropped.

"You've got it. Bring him in without stepping on the brakes to tip him off that we know he's back there. Are you sure you don't want to join my team?"

"Yeah." She shot him a grin and looked into the mirror, watching the distance close between them and the tail.

Up ahead the light turned yellow, then red.

Ava stepped on the brake and stopped, with the agent right behind them.

In one swift motion Carson swung around and squeezed off four rounds, hitting the car's radiator.

Steam hissed out of the holes.

She smashed down on the gas pedal. The car shot forward through the red light, leaving the rogue agent behind.

Relief rippled along her nerves as she signaled and entered the Georgetown turnpike.

"You could have killed him, couldn't you?"

"Yeah."

Emotions bunched in her chest as she brought the car up to speed. Carson Nash was all about control. He wasn't a relentless killer piling on the body count just for the heck of it. She knew that now. He could exercise his mercy at will.

A pocket of respect formed and seeped into her core along with an emotion she'd never felt before. Was it love?

"I want you to remove the chip from my back, Carson." She glanced over at him in the running shadows that surged and faded as they passed under the streetlights along the pike. "If we give Glendow the chip, he'll leave us alone."

The air in the car seemed to become charged with energy—positive or negative, she wasn't sure. She only knew her request had sparked something in him, and she could feel the coming storm.

"Glendow is a murderer, or have you forgotten? He knifed Jerome Hinshaw while you watched. There's no negotiating with a desperate man like him. Chip or no chip, we're both marked for death."

Ava sobered, suddenly wishing she'd

never considered the idea, but in her heart she wanted to believe this could be dragged to a conclusion they could live with. That somewhere down the line, she and Carson…and their child…could become a family.

"Please. Just think about it. We could remove the chip and hide it somewhere…get as far away as possible. Maybe even your team digs in Idaho. He won't kill us if we're the only ones who know where it is."

The silence in the car was deafening.

All the pleading in the world wasn't going to convince Carson, she knew that, but she held out hope anyway.

"Where are we going?" she asked, fed up with the quiet.

"Shopping mall, grocery store. Anywhere we can dump this car and catch a city bus."

"Okay." Worried, she considered their next move. They were out of options—not that they'd ever really had any. Glendow was a traitor. He'd probably banked the Russian's money in a Swiss account and if the deal had transpired as planned, he'd be all over it by now, and no one would have been the wiser.

Carson ground his teeth, fighting his own doubts. The details of Ava's suggestion needed modification, but there were aspects he could use. The risk was over the top. Glendow had been systematically killing off anyone who'd been party to the transaction. With Resnick and Hinshaw dead, there was only Ava and himself to be dealt with.

"I'll do it, Ava." He couldn't believe the words had come from his mouth, but he continued, drawing on his years of training to make it plausible.

"I'll remove the chip and hide it. We'll set up a dialogue with Glendow. If we're lucky, he'll take the deal and we'll make it out alive."

"It'll work, Carson," she said, a note of hope in her voice.

Carson clenched his jaw, a breath away from taking back the crazy idea and pulling her into his arms again, but he kept still. It would work.

It had to work.

They were out of options.

Chapter Fifteen

Ava watched Carson move the lighter's flame under the blade of his pocketknife.

She closed her eyes and took a deep breath, holding the queasiness in her stomach at bay for the moment.

It would be over soon, she reasoned. He would never intentionally hurt her—he had skills, for crying out loud. She didn't know if one of them was minor surgery, but she trusted him anyway.

"I wish I could tell you this isn't going to hurt."

Her eyes flew open and she considered him in the first light of morning breaking around their location under a tree in a small park beside the mall where they'd ditched the car.

"I'm having a hard enough time trying to psych myself up without that information."

"Sorry." He flipped the knife over to sterilize the other side of the blade.

She closed her eyes again. How was she ever going to survive labor and delivery if she couldn't handle what was to come. Gritting her teeth, she listened to Carson fiddle in his backpack and tried to relax.

The feel of his hands on the bare skin of her back sent a shiver through her.

"Some alcohol," he said, followed by a cold prep on her skin as he rubbed it over the spot where the microchip had been implanted.

"The initial incision is half an inch long. I'll follow the incision line. Hold still."

"I'm ready." Ava took several deep breaths and focused her mind on a snippet from her childhood, reliving the moment in her head over and over again until searing pain burned into her back, driving the happy memory into oblivion.

She gritted her teeth, trying not to react, not to move for fear of jostling the knife.

"Done...it's done." The sound of Carson's relief was obvious.

She hung her head, feeling his hands on her as he placed a gauze bandage over the incision and taped it in place.

"Let me see it." Reaching for her T-shirt, she pulled it down into place and turned toward Carson.

In the palm of his hand lay a tiny black square, covered in blood.

Ava swallowed against the tightness in her throat and resisted the urge to touch it. "That's what this is all about?"

"Yeah. It looks like a piece of plastic, but it's a bootleg chip with the power to reaim our entire spy satellite network."

She shuddered as she watched Carson close his fingers over it.

"We need to find a good place to hide it," she said, knowing it must never fall into enemy hands. "Someplace where it won't be—"

"I'm going to take care of it. Stay here. Keep your eyes open. I won't be long."

She stared at Carson for a moment, realizing his plan didn't include her. "But—"

"It's better if you don't know where it is. It's a matter of national security. Glendow won't be able to find it unless he comes through me."

Tears burned the backs of her eyelids, but she concealed the hurt his words had evoked inside her. In short, if Glendow did manage to take her, she'd be unable to tell him where the chip was, even if he tortured her for the information.

Carson watched horror pass across Ava's face as she realized the sacrifice she might have to make for her country.

His heart twisted in his chest. He reached for her, but she stepped back and sat down on the grass.

Resolve flooded his veins, but it couldn't douse the flame of self-loathing that burned inside him.

"I'll be back. Use the pistol if you have to." He turned and strode toward the rear of the mall, his emotions in knots and their future on the line.

Ava tried to relax by watching a string of cars pull into the mall parking lot. A walking club, she decided, as one by one women clad in sweats and tennis shoes climbed out of their cars and headed for the main entrance.

A normal life. She wanted a normal life for herself and her unborn child. When this was over she planned to go after that life with everything she had, but the ache in her heart belied the hope lodged there.

Would Carson be in it? Could he ever care about her the way she cared about him?

Footsteps behind her sent her heart rate up as she prepared to do emotional battle with him.

"Carson—"

A hand cupped over her mouth.

She tried to scream, but it was useless.

The assailant pulled her to her feet, dragging her backward across the grass.

Ava fought against the onslaught, but to no avail—he was too strong.

Shaking her head back and forth, she worked until she could bite down on his hand. He only squeezed harder.

In a matter of seconds he dragged her into a waiting van and closed the door.

The acceleration forced her to the floor along with her abductor.

Hope stirred in her as she broke free from his grasp, but the triumph was fleeting as the agent reacted by poking a pistol in her face.

Ava went still, staring down the barrel of the gun.

Director Glendow turned in the passenger seat and grinned at her. "Hello, Ava. You have something I want. Agent, do the honors, then kill her."

She tried to dodge the burly man, but he managed to shove her against the seat and pin her down. She lay still, catching her breath, planning for a rematch.

The man yanked her shirt up on her back. "You better look at this."

Director Glendow moved out of his seat and shuffled into the back. "Dammit." He ripped her bandage off.

Ava fought a cry of pain and braced for certain death.

"Where the hell is it, Ava?"

Fear knotted her nerves. She weighed the truth against a lie. Either way she was dead. Maybe she could buy some time.

"Agent Nash removed it."

The agent jerked her up into the seat.

She faced Glendow. Breathing heavily, she

regained her composure and stared back at him. A man she'd trusted, even liked until now.

"You killed Jerome Hinshaw in the back of the limo. I remember."

A brief look of surprise crossed his face and flashed in his dark eyes. "Three's a crowd. Hinshaw was brilliant, but he didn't figure into the money split."

"So you killed him and took his share."

"I knew you were bright, Agent Ross, but this conversation is done." He moved closer to her.

Fear screamed a warning into her brain just as Glendow grabbed her by the throat.

Ava tried to pull air into her lungs, fighting against his death grip. She clawed his hand, desperate to breathe.

He released her.

She pulled in a gasping breath, fighting dizziness.

"Tell me what he did with the microchip, or next time I won't stop squeezing. You don't want your baby to go without oxygen for too long, do you?"

Horror exploded inside her as she

searched his face for a measure of mercy, but it wasn't there. His features were hard and cold. His dark eyes were black holes of nothingness.

"I don't know what he did with it."

"That's a problem for you," Glendow said, leaning back against the seat. "Tell me, Ava, do you think he'll trade your life and his baby's life for that chip?"

Her heart ripped in her chest, torn apart by Glendow's question. Had Carson known she'd be sacrificed if he ever took her? Wouldn't she be sacrificed either way?

She fought a sob as it rattled up her throat. "No."

Glendow cocked his head and narrowed his eyes. "We'll have to see."

Ava released the tears burning the backs of her eyelids and stared out the window of the moving van.

Had she only imagined the feelings between them? Or was she still just a package in Carson Nash's mission?

CARSON RACED for the grassy park where he'd left Ava.

In the parking lot he'd spotted the car

they'd ditched being swarmed by agents. He guessed Glendow had tagged it with GPS back at the apartment, which explained why the agent tailing them hadn't been in any particular hurry.

This was a storm they couldn't outrun, and there weren't any more places to hide.

Panic shot through him as he rounded the corner, staring at the patch of grass where he'd left her a moment ago.

It was empty.

Rage sliced into him. He sprinted onto the knoll, catching sight of the drag marks across the grass. His heart pounded, and he prayed his plan worked. That he hadn't just made the biggest miscalculation of his life.

His cell rang. He pulled the phone from his belt and answered without even a glance at the screen. "Hello."

"Agent Nash. Nice to hear the voice of the man who's given me so much trouble."

Carson's nerves tightened, and his hearing went on high alert.

"Glendow?"

"You have something I want, if Agent Ross is to be believed."

"If you hurt her, you'll never get the chip from me."

"So you're willing to make a trade?"

"When and where?" Carson was careful to regulate the tone of his voice. "But only after I know for sure she's still alive. Put her on the phone."

"Carson?" Ava whispered into the cell, but before he could answer he heard Glendow's voice again.

"Great Falls Park, north of McLean. Overlook three. Four o'clock. Come alone and unarmed. If I see anybody but you, she's dead." Glendow hung up.

Carson closed his cell phone. His head drooped forward as a rush of emotion raged through his body.

Ava was still alive.

His plan was working.

CARSON STARED at the waters of the Potomac as they cascaded over the falls one hundred feet upstream.

He glanced at his watch. Three-forty.

Picking up his pace, he reached overlook three and walked out onto the upper deck. In less than twenty minutes his life would change, one way or another.

The afternoon air was still, the heat dissipated only by the shade of the trees surrounding the platform. The park was virtually empty. Maybe the hikers and bikers had decided to stay inside where it was cool.

He went to the railing and turned, leaning against it in a casual manner as he stared out at the landscape, looking for signs of movement among the trees and brush.

The river at his back offered a barrier he hoped Glendow took for granted. Reaching up, he brushed his hand over his head.

He'd spent the day working the scenario in his brain until he'd convinced himself every avenue had been considered and explored. But still, he couldn't eradicate the worry that wreaked havoc on his emotions.

He was in love with Ava Ross, and all the planning and preparation on the planet might not save her. It made the knowledge that he could lose her in an instant all the more devastating.

Gazing at the trail meandering past the overlook, he caught sight of movement through the dense forest a few yards to the south.

His muscles knotted with tension as he focused on a single individual walking along the trail.

A glint of sunshine through the canopy of leaves glanced off Ava's mahogany hair.

His heart thundered in his chest. Something was wrong. She was alone.

Where was Glendow?

Carson stepped away from the rail, eager to get to her, protect her, but he froze in place as she moved off the path and stopped just short of the overlook deck.

He moved toward her.

She raised her hand. "Stop! Don't come any closer."

Confusion clouded his mind as he stared at her face.

There was no color in her cheeks. Her body trembled so much that he could see her shake.

"Where's Glendow?"

She didn't reply to his question, but instead reached down and gingerly pulled open the oversize white shirt she wore.

Carson's gut squeezed.

Cold hard reality slammed into his brain, unleashing his worst fears like a bag of poisonous snakes.

His stare locked on Ava's waist, on the block of C4 skewed with a probe detonator.

Fear coiled around his body, squeezing the breath out of his lungs.

She'd been wired with explosives.

Chapter Sixteen

Ava tried to breathe as beads of sweat formed at the nape of her neck and rolled down her back in rivulets she was too frightened to brush away for fear of setting off the bomb attached to her body.

Panic set in as she stared at Carson.

"Where is he?" he asked, taking a step toward her.

She swallowed. "He left me on the trail, but I don't know if he's there anymore."

"Are you wearing a wire?"

"No."

Carson took another step toward her.

She fought the need to bolt, to protect him from being blown to bits if she could. "Please...don't get too close," she begged.

"You know I will. It's the only way."

A choked sob rose in her throat. "I can't let you...I love you." She took a step back.

"You've got no choice, sweetheart, because I love you, too, and Glendow won't risk destroying the chip by detonating the bomb. We've got a better chance together."

She stared at him, feeling a zing of hope.

In three steps Carson reached her. Putting out his hand, he stroked her cheek and stared into her eyes.

"Nitro, do you copy?" he said into his hidden microphone, still staring at her, still touching her. "We've got a problem."

Confusion contorted her face, pulling her brows together.

Carson increased the pressure against her cheek. "If Glendow is watching he needs to believe we're speaking to one another."

Ava nodded.

"Loud and clear, Marathon. Go ahead."

Glancing down, he studied the bomb strapped around her midsection.

"I'm looking at a simple C4 quarter brick with a probe detonator. Two wires, one red, one white."

"Copy. Clip the red wire one-half inch from the head of the probe."

His cell rang.

Carson pulled it from his belt, letting his hand drop from Ava's face. "Yeah."

"Do you like my insurance policy?" Glendow's self-assured voice sounded at the other end of the line. "I don't trust you, Nash. Leave her there and follow my instruction. Now, take a step back or I'll set it off."

He stepped closer, prepared to play Russian roulette.

"If she goes, I go, and so does the microchip."

Silence filled the airspace between him and Glendow.

His nerves stretched tight. Had he made the right call?

"Take the river trail and head east. At an eighth of a mile in, you'll come to a picnic area surrounded by trees. Wait there for my call. And Nash, I'll be watching every step you take. Don't try anything, or she and the kid die."

Rage coursed through Carson. "You know about the baby?"

"Resnick told me she was pregnant. I put you two together the night before she left D.C. with a DNA sample from her bedroom."

"I'm not buying it."

"I saw the way she stared up at the bedroom window, and I saw your profile behind the curtain. It was easy to collect DNA—the damn stuff was everywhere. The match came up in-house. The only thing I couldn't predict was that you'd be sent into the field to rescue her from the Russians."

Carson swallowed his anger and sobered. He may have been given pertinent details, but they weren't in the clear yet.

Far from it.

"You're a son of a bitch, Glendow."

Carson closed the phone, watching a single tear slide down Ava's cheek.

"We can do this, babe."

She closed her eyes for a moment. When she opened them again he could see determination where fear had been only moments before.

"I'm ready. Which way?" She turned and walked back up onto the trail.

"East." Carson followed close behind her looking for his opportunity. It came in the form of a woman jogging with her leashed dog. At the last minute Carson stepped left and tripped over the dog. He hit the ground on his belly and jammed his hand into his pocket, retrieving his nail clippers.

"Oh, my gosh! Are you okay?"

The woman knelt next to him, while her dog licked his face.

"Yeah." Carson pulled himself to his feet, dusting the dirt and debris from his pants. "My fault."

He patted the friendly Irish setter and straightened. "Sorry about that." He nodded to the dog's owner and caught up with Ava, who'd paused less than three feet farther up the trail.

He could almost feel Glendow's eyes on them from somewhere in the woods, assessing the dog-crash scenario. He tensed, moved in closer to Ava and took her hand.

"Let's move." The hair at his nape bristled, but he kept his eyes on the trail ahead.

"I have a pair of nail clippers. Can you

feel them?" He squeezed them against her palm.

"Ouch."

"Good." Carson spotted the river trail sign and broke left onto it. "Listen to me carefully. I want you to use them to clip the red wire one-half inch from the top of the probe. Do it exactly as I said."

He glanced over at her, felt her hesitate for a moment before nodding. "Red wire, one-half inch from the probe." She repeated his instructions.

"We'll keep moving. Drop back half a step. Use my body as cover. Glendow is probably watching from the woods to the right of us. Then button the shirt."

Carson swallowed, feeling her pull against his grip as she removed the clippers, transferring them into her left hand before regrasping his.

Ava's heart pounded in her chest and echoed in her eardrums as she put one foot in front of the other, dropping a half step back next to Carson.

Numbing calm took her nerves as she stared down at the explosive nightmare belted around her waist. With the clippers in hand she raised them to the red wire. One-half inch. She mentally repeated the distance and clamped down.

Click. The red wire snapped.

She pulled in a breath and shoved the clippers into her pants pocket. "It's done." Taking her hand out of Carson's, she buttoned the last three buttons on the oversize shirt.

Carson tried to relax. The bomb had been defused, hadn't it? His team was waiting to take Glendow out, so why couldn't he eliminate the worry wreaking havoc on his nerves?

The trail narrowed and darkened as the trees and underbrush grew more dense around them.

He moved Ava in behind him, picking his way closer to the clearing Glendow had described.

Together they walked into a circle of trees with a picnic table in the center.

The rustle of brush on their left put Carson in attack mode.

Director Glendow stepped out of the underbrush, a small black detonator in his hand.

"I'll take that chip now," he said, keeping his distance from both of them.

Cautiously Carson raised his hand and reached into his shirt pocket, pulling out a small plastic bag. "Hand over the detonator and the microchip is yours."

Glendow gave him a wary smirk. "You first, Nash. Put the chip on the table unless you want to see her scrambled."

Carson hesitated. Once Glendow got a good look at the chip, the jig was up. "I don't trust you. We'll do it together or not at all."

An instant of greed glittered in Glendow's black eyes. He took a step forward.

Carson matched him movement for movement until they both stood at the table.

He tossed the bag and whirled left, catching Glendow in the face with a right hook.

Glendow stumbled backward, anger burning in his eyes. "She dies!" he bellowed.

Before Carson could stop him, Glendow pressed the button on the detonator.

Milliseconds passed like hours as he

stared in Ava's direction, praying they'd defused the bomb for certain.

Glendow blanched.

Carson charged him, taking him to the ground.

The shuffle of boots filled Carson's ears as he drove his fist into Glendow's face again and again.

"Stand down, Agent!" an unfamiliar voice shouted from somewhere in the clearing.

"Nash!"

The sound of Mark Jarrett's holler sliced into his brain.

He stopped his fist just short of the director's face for the last time and stood up, searching for Ava among the team.

Agent Jarrett was busy removing the bomb belt from her waist.

Agent Shelby pulled the director to his feet and frisked him for weapons as Agents Hunt and Carico strode in from the surrounding woods, sniper rifles in hand.

He focused on Ava, moving toward her like a man on fire.

Wrapping his arms around her, he buried his face against her neck.

"You SOB," Glendow yelled, staring at the bag lying on the picnic table next to where Agent Shelby had made him sit in handcuffs. "It's a piece of plastic!"

Carson stepped toward him, unable to keep the grin off his face. "You had the microchip the whole time. From the minute you took her. I never removed it. I just made you believe I had in order to keep her alive."

Ava squeezed Carson's hand as his admission sank into her brain. How could she ever have doubted him? Her heart squeezed in her chest as he pulled her closer, wrapping his arm around her waist.

"Agent Nash." A man in a suit stepped in front of them. "I'm Agent Morallis, NSA. You're a hard man to catch up to."

"I wasn't aware there was any cooperation between our two entities, Agent."

"Not until now. We've been onto Director Glendow, Dr. Resnick and Jerome Hinshaw for months. Hinshaw's body turned up last week in Maryland, but it was his research that got our attention. You have my thanks for recovering the microchip and detaining Director Glendow."

"You're welcome."

"Agent Ross." He turned his attention to Ava. "If you'll come with me, we'll take you to the medical center and have the chip removed."

Ava smiled. Her ordeal was almost over, short of a minor incision—one accompanied by anesthetic this time.

"I'll be along in a minute," she said.

"Take your time." The NSA agent moved away to speak with one of his men.

Carson pointed Ava toward the circle where his team stood, stowing their gear. "There are some guys I want you to meet. You were unconscious the last time they saw you."

Heat flamed in her cheeks, turning them a shade of pink that only served to raise the desire level in his body.

"Mission accomplished." He stepped into the group. "This was off the record and risky, but you came through for us."

"That's what we're here for," Agent Mark Jarrett said, his gaze roaming between the two of them before a knowing grin parted his lips.

Introductions went around and the four men dispersed, leaving Ava and Carson to follow behind the group as they hiked the trail to the parking lot.

Seeing the perfect opening, Carson pulled Ava into the brush and pinned her against a tree.

Staring into her eyes, he lowered his mouth to hers, tasting her like a starving man.

Brushing his hand down her body, he stopped and spread his fingers over her belly. He ended the kiss and smiled at her, his heart on fire.

"What I said back at the overlook—I meant every word of it. I love you, Ava, and our child, sight unseen." A moment of hesitation held up his words, but he broke through the mental barriers he'd learned to erect around his emotions. He never wanted a life without her in it.

"The CIA is what I do, but there's room for more…. For us. Will you have me?"

Ava relaxed, letting the total-man-dominance thing sweep her into ecstasy. She could live in his testosterone-saturated world. In fact, there wasn't anywhere else she'd rather be, now or forever.

"Yes," she said, laying her head against his chest. She breathed him in, feeling a brief quickening deep inside her as their child let its presence be felt.

Leaning back, she gazed into his eyes and brushed her fingertips over the deep scar above his left eyebrow, his hallmark of sorts.

"I love you, too, Carson. And even if you don't believe it yet, I know you're going to be a great husband and father. It's in your DNA."

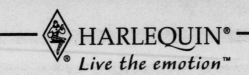
HARLEQUIN®
Live the emotion™

The series you love are now available in
LARGER PRINT!

The books are complete and unabridged—
printed in a larger type size to make it
easier on your eyes.

HARLEQUIN®

HARLEQUIN ROMANCE®
From the Heart, For the Heart

HARLEQUIN®
INTRIGUE
Breathtaking Romantic Suspense

HARLEQUIN®
Presents
Seduction and Passion Guaranteed!

HARLEQUIN®
Super Romance®
Exciting, Emotional, Unexpected

Try LARGER PRINT today!
Visit: www.eHarlequin.com
Call: 1-800-873-8635

HLPDIR07

HARLEQUIN ROMANCE®

The rush of falling in love,

Cosmopolitan, international settings,

Believable, feel-good stories about today's women

The compelling thrill of romantic excitement

It could happen to you!

EXPERIENCE HARLEQUIN ROMANCE!

Available wherever Harlequin Books are sold.

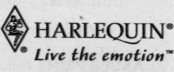

HARLEQUIN®
Live the emotion™

www.eHarlequin.com

HROMDIR04

HARLEQUIN®

American ROMANCE®

Invites *you* to experience lively, heartwarming all-American romances

Every month, we bring you four strong, sexy men, and four women who know what they want—and go all out to get it.

From small towns to big cities, experience a sense of adventure, romance and family spirit—the all-American way!

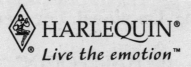

American ROMANCE
Heart, Home & Happiness

HARLEQUIN®
Live the emotion™

www.eHarlequin.com   HARDIR06

HARLEQUIN®

Super Romance®

...there's more to the story!

Superromance.

A *big* satisfying read about unforgettable characters. Each month we offer *six* very different stories that range from family drama to adventure and mystery, from highly emotional stories to romantic comedies—and much more! Stories about people you'll believe in and care about. Stories too compelling to put down....

Our authors are among today's *best* romance writers. You'll find familiar names and talented newcomers. Many of them are award winners—and you'll see why!

If you want the biggest and best in romance fiction, you'll get it from Superromance!

Exciting, Emotional, Unexpected...

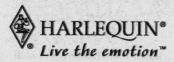

HARLEQUIN®
Live the emotion™

www.eHarlequin.com   HSDIR06

HARLEQUIN®
Presents

The world's bestselling romance series...
The series that brings you your favorite authors,
month after month:

Helen Bianchin...Emma Darcy
Lynne Graham...Penny Jordan
Miranda Lee...Sandra Marton
Anne Mather...Carole Mortimer
Susan Napier...Michelle Reid

and many more uniquely talented authors!

Wealthy, powerful, gorgeous men...
Women who have feelings just like your own...
The stories you love, set in exotic, glamorous locations...

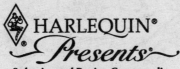

HARLEQUIN®
Presents

Seduction and Passion Guaranteed!

www.eHarlequin.com

HPDIR104

Harlequin® Historical
Historical Romantic Adventure!

Imagine a time of chivalrous knights and unconventional ladies, roguish rakes and impetuous heiresses, rugged cowboys and spirited frontierswomen— these rich and vivid tales will capture your imagination!

Harlequin Historical . . . they're too good to miss!

www.eHarlequin.com

HHDIR06

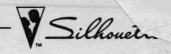

Silhouette
SPECIAL EDITION™

Emotional, compelling stories that capture the intensity of living, loving and creating a family in today's world.

Silhouette
Desire

Modern, passionate reads that are powerful and provocative.

Silhouette
nocturne

Dramatic and sensual tales of paranormal romance.

Silhouette Romantic
SUSPENSE

Romances that are sparked by danger and fueled by passion.

Visit Silhouette Books at www.eHarlequin.com

V *Silhouette*

SPECIAL EDITION™

Emotional, compelling stories that capture the intensity of living, loving and creating a family in today's world.

Special Edition features bestselling authors such as Susan Mallery, Sherryl Woods, Christine Rimmer, Joan Elliott Pickart— and many more!

For a romantic, complex and emotional read, choose Silhouette Special Edition.

Visit Silhouette Books at www.eHarlequin.com

SSEGEN06